LIA PARK

PARK

AND THE HEAVENLY HEIRLOOMS

Also by Jenna Yoon

Lia Park and the Missing Jewel

LIA PARK
AND THE HEAVENLY HEIRLOOMS

JENNA YOON

ALADDIN

NEW YORK LONDON TORONTO SYDNEY NEW DELHI

ALADDIN

An imprint of Simon & Schuster Children's Publishing Division
1230 Avenue of the Americas, New York, New York 10020
First Aladdin hardcover edition May 2023
Text copyright © 2023 by Jenna Yoon
Jacket illustration copyright © 2023 by Hyuna Lee
All rights reserved, including the right of
reproduction in whole or in part in any form.
ALADDIN and related logo are registered trademarks of Simon & Schuster, Inc.
For information about special discounts for bulk purchases, please contact Simon & Schuster Special Sales at 1-866-506-1949 or business@simonandschuster.com.
The Simon & Schuster Speakers Bureau can bring authors to your live event. For more information or to book an event contact the Simon & Schuster Speakers Bureau at 1-866-248-3049 or visit our website at www.simonspeakers.com.
Jacket designed by Heather Palisi
Interior designed by Ginny Kemmerer
The text of this book was set in ITC Usherwood Std.
Manufactured in the United States of America 0423 FFG
2 4 6 8 10 9 7 5 3 1
Library of Congress Control Number 2022950388
ISBN 9781534487963 (hc)
ISBN 9781534487987 (ebook)

For Mihee and Taehee, my little 충전기들

Saranghae always and forever

Chapter 1

It had been the longest summer break ever, but the day I had been looking forward to practically all my life was finally here. The International Magic Agency sponsored a school for kids with magic and trained them to protect the world from monsters. Yes, they did exist, and some of them were a threat to humanity. The name of the school was—wait for it—International Magic School. They kept the first two initials the same, to avoid confusion with the names for the normal people's government bureaus. All students were required to board there, so of course I'd spent every last second I had packing, unpacking, and then repacking all my stuff to make extra sure I had everything I needed.

For security reasons, parents were only allowed to visit on designated days. It was nerve-racking to be apart from them for this long, but I was still excited that I'd be living on my own. I could almost taste the sweetness of my newfound freedom.

I craned my neck and peeked between the two front seats. Just like the last time I checked, we were still on the main road in the city of Yongin, which was about an hour outside of Seoul, where we lived with my halmoni. We'd just entered through the Mabuk-dong neighborhood.

"Make a left at the next light," Umma instructed from the front passenger seat.

Appa laughed as he flicked on his blinker. "Don't worry, yeobo. I have a photographic memory, remember?"

She hit his arm lightly. "Yet you always miss the turns."

Appa reached over to hold her hand. "You're right. I'd be so lost without you."

Oh, Appa. Always the corny one. Though lately he had taken it up a notch and transformed into the king of dad jokes. Married people called each other *yeobo*, but my parents used to say it only when they were in a good mood. But ever since we moved back to Korea, they said it, like, after every other sentence.

The second our plane landed here, the tenseness in Umma's face melted away. She didn't need to explain why because I knew.

We no longer needed to live in fear of being caught.

And that made all the difference.

Once we'd turned left, we headed down a narrow, dusty farm road that led us straight toward Beophwa-san. Seventy percent of Korea was made up of san—mountains—which was why they were pretty hard to miss wherever you went.

Appa looked at me in the rearview mirror. "Uri Lia, jal chamne."

"Thanks, Appa." I giggled and clasped my hands on top of my lap. "You may now call me Queen Patience."

Younger me would've asked them every ten minutes if we were there yet, but this new and improved first-year student at IMS would never. I had better self-control than that now.

Umma flashed a double thumbs-up above her headrest. "Geuroge uri Lia da keonne."

Totally agreed. I was very mature now.

"Can I go to the Jay One concert by myself, then?"

"Nice try," Umma said. "You're not that grown-up yet."

It was worth asking. I mean, who knew, maybe

someday she'd cave and let me go with my friends. Her overprotectiveness didn't even bother me anymore, because I had something so much better waiting for me, exploring the school with my best friend, Joon. I still couldn't believe it was finally happening and we had made it.

I adjusted a few strands of my hair to cover the white streak and used two black bobby pins to hold it all in place. Then I tied my hair in a ponytail.

Hair camouflage mode activated.

Appa looked back at me at the red light. "You don't have to hide it."

Actually, yes, I did. I'd dyed it and even colored it with a black permanent marker, with zero success. As a last resort, using a pair of scissors, I'd snipped off the white streak.

What had happened next had almost made me cry.

It had grown back and looked whiter than before. As it turned out, magical marks couldn't really be covered. So my best bet was to hide it under my regular black hair.

"I think it looks cool," Umma said.

My parents' opinions were not to be 100 percent trusted, because of course they'd think their own kid looked good.

I double-checked in the mirror to make sure my disguise was secured in place. "I just don't want to have to explain to every single person I meet."

Was it so bad that I wanted kids to like me for me and not be judged for what I'd done? Or be singled out as "that girl"? No, thank you. I planned to hide it for as long as possible.

At the end of the road, a two-story building with large windows spaced close together stood at the base of an enormous mountain. Our car tires crunched over the gravel as we drove onto an empty dirt field and parked.

The sign above the main entrance read *International Mabuk School.*

Uh. Definitely not the right school.

Appa should've paid more attention to Umma's directions instead of relying just on his photographic memory.

Where were we?

Umma and Appa got out of the car.

Were we lost? And were they asking for directions? But they didn't seem worried at all.

Appa popped open the trunk and lugged my suitcase out.

Umma opened my door. "Come on, we're going to be late."

Was it just me, or did they really not see that we were at the wrong place?

I pointed to the sign ahead. "This is Mabuk School, not Magic School."

Umma unfastened my seat belt and winked. "All part of the cloaking mechanism."

Interesting. If what she said was true, this was a next-level hidden-in-plain-sight strategy.

When I stepped out of the car, the silence was deafening. Not a bird in the sky. I couldn't hear any kids' voices.

I blinked a few times and lasered in on the sign above the door. I half expected the letters to morph, rearrange, or change into the correct name of the school.

Conclusion: not an enchanted sign.

Inside, against the wall facing me stood two large purple orchids on each side of a tall water feature made of different-sized rocks. A security guard in a navy-blue uniform sat behind a booth right next to the entrance.

"Eotteoke osyeosseubnikka?"

Umma took out her wallet and slid across their driver's licenses and the identification card that I had received in the welcome packet. "We're here to drop off our daughter."

I raised my hand and bowed. My smile was met with

the most expressionless face I'd ever seen. He could've passed for an AI.

He checked his watch. "You're the first ones here."

Of course we were. Because to Umma, *on time* and *late* meant the same thing. One of the most valuable tools for an agent was time, which couldn't be bought with money, only earned by arriving early. So she had stuck to this motto my entire life.

The guard took all our IDs and scooted a rectangular reader in our direction. "Place your index finger on top."

I frowned because this all looked very ordinary—in fact, the farthest thing from magic possible. Fingerprint readers were used everywhere.

Umma pressed her finger on it, and then Appa, who passed it to me. I placed my finger on it, and a green light moved up and down.

I stayed quiet as the guard stared at the computer screen in front of him.

Seconds crawled by.

Finally he smiled and gestured toward the door next to the plant on the right. "Welcome, Lia Park."

I bowed and said, "Gamsahabnida."

This time he actually waved and grinned. "You're welcome. Have a great time here."

Before following Umma and Appa out the door, I snuck into the hallway. I didn't know what I expected to see, but for sure it wasn't actual classrooms with desks, chairs, books, and a whiteboard. This setup reminded me of the classrooms at West Hills Middle School back in California. The most normal people school ever.

"Lia ya," Umma called out. "Come on!"

"Ne!" I raced through the door that Appa propped open for me.

And stopped dead in my tracks.

Right in front of my face was tall grass that towered over me. It was everywhere, as far as I could see. We couldn't move away from the door because there was nowhere to go.

I pulled the grass to the sides to try to squeeze through.

It snapped back and hit me.

I yelped and jumped back.

What kind of grass slaps people?

Appa held my shoulder. "Watch this."

Umma pressed her face close and stroked the grass. "Yaedeula gil jom mandeuleo jugettni?"

I stopped myself from laughing out loud because I didn't want to be rude. But Umma was talking to the grass in a tone she used to speak to little kids.

The grass giggled and parted just enough for us to take five steps.

It did exactly what she had asked it to do—the grass made a path for us.

Umma patted the grass. "Gomawo. Sugohaesseo."

I copied her and let my hand rest on top of the grass. "Thanks and good job."

It weaved around my leg and nuzzled like a cat would. So cute. No wonder Umma talked to the grass like that.

We walked in a single file down the narrow path, Umma, me, and then Appa. The grass rustled and opened up with each step Umma took and closed the path behind Appa.

Because the grass was so tall, I couldn't see anything else in front of me. "So is this the way to the school?"

"Yes," Umma said. "But it'll make more sense once you see it."

I'd just have to take her word for it. On to the next question, then. "How come the sign at the front of the school is wrong?"

"When you're out in the normal-people world and someone asks you where you go to school," Appa explained, "how will you answer?"

Hmmm. Excellent point. One of the most basic rules

of IMA was to keep our identities hidden from normal people.

"So this is all a cover?"

"Now you're catching on," Appa said. "It's an accredited school, so you'll be getting your high school diploma from here."

That was brilliant. Now I really felt like a spy from the movies with a full undercover operation.

Umma passed me my identification card. "Have a look."

I took the card from her and did a double take.

The card had changed.

When I'd given Umma my card this morning, it had said under my picture, *International Magic School, Student: Lia Park, House of Benevolence.* Now it read *International Mabuk School, Student: Lia Park, Grade 7.* On the other side of the card was an address and phone number.

"So don't forget to keep this with you whenever you're out in the normal-people world," Appa said.

About ten minutes later the path opened up completely and we came face-to-face with two blue stone haetae statues on pedestals. They stood in front of a small grove of trees at the base of the mountain.

Haetae was a mythological creature that had the body of a lion, scales, a bell around its neck, and a flattened horn on its head.

Wherever the school was, I felt so much safer having these haetae statues around, even if they weren't real. These guardian lions were said to have protected places from disaster and warded off evil spirits.

Appa placed inside the left haetae's mouth a round chip that had come in the welcome package.

And we waited.

CHAPTER 2

In the distance, a guard in a light blue button-down shirt and dark pants strolled out from behind the trees. He placed a dark blue cap on his head, and turned it once to the right, then the left, and back to the center again. I couldn't make out the gold letters on the front of the cap, but they began to shimmer.

The trees closest to us faded away, and in their place a massive stone foundation appeared. On top of it was a traditional Korean gate with red pillars and a roof that curved up at the ends. A rectangular panel with the words *International Magic School* attached itself to the center of the horizontal beams right below the roof.

The gate with its red pillars, and blue and green patterns on the roof, blended harmoniously with the giant lush trees surrounding it. The school was hidden from sight by the billowy trees that created a tunnel covering a brick road that led inside.

This must've been what Appa had meant earlier. I knew I was a real part of the IMA world now, but witnessing a school appear out of thin air was still supercool. "Just as I remembered," Umma said. "Top-notch security."

Appa stood under the gate and gazed up. "Lia, do you see all the decorations?"

There were so many patterns and colors that I didn't know where to start. I focused on one area with wave patterns in orange, yellow, black, blue, green, and red. Painted right next to it was a green leaf motif with flowers.

"So intricate and pretty," I marveled.

Umma joined us. "This type of decoration on temples, palaces, and gates is called dancheong."

"Did you know that special painters called dancheong-jang, who have been designated as a national Intangible Cultural Heritage, are the only ones allowed to work on it?" Appa said.

His photographic memory came in very handy at times like this.

"And each person was in charge of one color only," Umma added.

I stared up at the roof again. It was so detailed and colorful. Simply stunning. "I bet it took them a really long time."

Appa chuckled. "Sure did." When the guard finally approached us, Umma's face lit up. She ran up to greet him and held his hand.

"Ajeossi! Neomu oraenmanieyo."

Appa bowed and said, "It has been so long."

The guard studied their faces for a moment and then broke out into a smile. "It can't be. Chung Mira? Park Minwoo?"

Umma threw her arms around him in a big hug. "Ne, jeohuieyo."

"I never thought I'd see you two again," he said, patting her back. "The great invincible duo who no one expected to die."

She pulled away and put her arm around my shoulders. "And this is our daughter, Lia. She'll be a First Year."

"Let's see. Bungeoppangine."

That was literally the name of a fish-shaped pastry filled with red bean paste. A very popular Korean street food snack in the winter. But because the pastries were pressed into molds, the bungeoppang looked exactly like each other, which became a second meaning for that phrase.

Everyone I met always said I was Umma's mini-me. But I just didn't see it. Maybe I looked like she had when she was my age, but I didn't think we looked anything like each other right now. The only thing we had in common was our straight black hair? Though I hoped to look like her when I got older.

The guard took my suitcase and placed it against a tree. "Which house?"

"Same as me," Umma said. "House of Benevolence."

He placed a tag with an image of a blue dragon on my suitcase. "Perfect match, I'm sure."

"Where do I go to pick up my bag?" I asked.

"To your house, of course." The guard tapped twice on the side of the only tree with red leaves, and it opened up, revealing a large conveyor belt. Then the tree sucked up my suitcase and it disappeared.

"Head down to the lawn," he said. "Eotteoke ganeunji gieoknaji?"

Umma smiled and bowed. "Of course I remember how to get there."

Appa whispered into my ear, "He's the first line of defense in protecting the school."

The guard didn't seem very powerful at all. I didn't know

exactly how old he was, but if he had been around when my parents were in school, now he must have been over sixty years old. It was hard to picture him battling intruders. At IMS most people spoke fluent Korean, English, or Konglish, which was mixing both languages together. Thank goodness my parents had forced me to learn Korean, or I'd have had a hard time understanding these conversations.

I followed Umma as she led the way. Except for a fairly wide paved walkway, everywhere else had grass and trees. It almost felt like we were in the middle of a park. It was early September, so the leaves hadn't quite turned yet, and the fall weather was perfect, not too hot and not too cold.

"What if normal people end up here?"

"First of all, it's almost impossible to get through the grass," Appa explained. "And even if by some miracle they did, they'd just see trees and the mountain."

"Certain IMA-designated locations have a protection spell like this," Umma added.

No wonder Umma had no problems sending me here to live on my own. This place was a magic fortress, with basically nobody going in or out once school started.

When we reached a fork in the road, Umma pointed to the left. "That's where the Hwarang training center is." Hwarangdo was a secret style of martial arts that was practiced only by Hwarangs, like Umma and me. Except I hadn't learned any moves yet. Umma wanted me to wait until school started to learn the basics properly with the master. It was a completely different style from Taekkyeon, which was what everyone had to learn to get into IMS.

From here I couldn't see the training center at all, but I couldn't wait to start. "Do I get to go every day?"

Umma stroked my hair. "It's every morning before school, except the weekend."

Oh no. I wasn't a morning riser at all. "How early?"

"It was so long ago," she said. "But maybe around six a.m.?"

Yikes. I'd never woken up at that time before, but it'd be okay: I had a plan. I took out my new smartphone that my parents had given me and immediately set alarms for five o'clock, five fifteen, and five thirty.

Appa hugged me tight. "You're so grown-up now. Look at you, making your backup plans."

"We taught her well." Umma high-fived Appa, and they continued to stroll down the path.

We didn't have to walk very far until we got to a large building that was shaped like a bird with its wings spread open. It was absolutely beautiful and looked impossible to create, because there was so much detail and the edges of the bird were so smooth, like a sculpture. No one would've guessed that this was a building.

"Is that the House of Courage?" I already knew the answer, because it was just so obviously the red-vermilion bird that was their symbol. This must have been where Joon would be staying. When we'd gotten our acceptance packages a few months ago, Joon had been thrilled and joked that he could now soar to new heights.

"Magnificent, isn't it?" Appa said. "That's what building with magic-infused materials can get you."

All of a sudden, the little tree house I had in my backyard didn't seem that great. "I'd like to request one of these in our new home."

Appa chuckled. "Maybe when we're billionaires. That kind of material costs a fortune."

A little bit past the building was a sculpture of the red-vermilion bird, spinning above what resembled an entrance to a subway station with stairs leading down.

"What in the world?" Umma said. "That wasn't here when we went to school."

As much as I wanted to hurry up and find Joon, I couldn't resist. "Can we check it out, please?"

Umma looked at the time on her phone. "We do have some time before the initiation ceremony starts."

I squealed, so excited to go on one last adventure together before my parents had to leave. Being an early bird paid off at times like this because we had a built-in time buffer. But no matter how thrilling all this was, I was going to miss them a lot.

I headed down the stairs but slammed into an invisible wall.

"I don't know how to get in," I said.

Once Umma faced the front of the giant statue, laser beams shot out and scanned her. Then the eyes glowed red. "I think it's ready now."

She went through and waited for me at the bottom of the stairs.

My turn. I stepped in front of the bird and froze. A second later, laser beams pointed at my sneakers and moved their way up my body. I twitched because they actually tickled a little. When the eyes turned red, I waved and said, "Thank you, birdie."

I bounded down the stairs and paused for a moment to take in what was in front of me. This was no ordinary subway station. A large translucent tube was suspended in the air where the track should've been.

Appa passed me and hurried down to the platform. "Let's go. You'll miss the ride."

I followed close behind him and Umma. We stopped behind the yellow line painted on the ground.

The side of the tube facing me slid up and opened, revealing a sleek silver train. Without warning, the doors of the train broke up into tiny squares, like pixels on an image. One by one the squares blinked and faded away, unmasking the interior of the train. Rows of seats faced in one direction. I couldn't believe we had this in our school.

The shape of the tube and the way the seats were arranged were unmistakably unique to hyperloops, which were basically supercharged high-speed trains stuffed inside gigantic tubes. The tubes were the train tracks.

I stepped inside the empty train and sat down on a smooth leather chair with armrests.

Umma and Appa plopped down on either side of me. The doors rolled down, and my body moved forward ever so slightly when the train took off.

"Can you believe how lucky these kids are?" Umma tightened my seat belt.

"A glorified shuttle bus," Appa said.

Umma laughed. "We didn't even have that."

A voice on the speaker said, "House of Strength," and the doors opened.

It felt like only a minute or two had passed since we'd

sat down. "How long would that have taken if we'd walked?"

"About ten to fifteen minutes?" Appa said.

So that confirmed what I had been thinking. This was definitely a mini hyperloop right in our own school. I'd never been in one before, so I looked forward to riding this every single day.

Umma leaned over me to talk to Appa. "Do you remember how we used to trudge to class when it snowed?"

Appa laughed so hard, he snorted. "How could I forget that time you came to class looking like a snowman."

This must be what old people did when they came back to their school a million years after they'd graduated. I promised myself that if I were ever to have kids someday, I'd never say things like that.

After we had circled around the entire school, we exited near the front entrance of the main academic building. We crossed a lawn that was covered in ten rows of white chairs, with five chairs on each side of the aisle that led to a table with stacks of uniforms tied in red bows, wallets, and a box of blank rectangular badges. Behind the table were a staircase leading up to the building and a sculpture of a large globe, with the letters *IMS* swirling around it.

Attached to the back of each seat was a piece of paper

with a name on it. The names didn't seem to be in any particular order. Definitely not alphabetized. But some last names were placed together in small groups of two or three.

Dozens of parents and kids walked around, greeting each other or searching for their names.

A woman dressed in a dark pink skirt and cream-colored blouse, with a neat ribbon tied around her neck, speed-walked toward us in heels. Umma and Appa noticed her and waved.

"I can't believe it's really you!" The woman hugged Umma and then stepped back a little. "How is it that you look exactly the same?"

Umma laughed. "You look great too! And you're a headmaster now!"

"Geureokke dwaesseo."

"It just happened?" Umma squeezed her shoulders. "You're still so modest. Becoming the head of a school takes a lot more than that."

"Look who's talking," she said. "IMA's legendary agents."

"After all you went through, you really deserve it," Umma said. "I'm so happy for you."

"They used to be inseparable when they went to school here," Appa whispered. "But we had to cut contact with everyone except a handful of people when we moved to California."

No wonder my parents were so excited to be back in Korea. Seeing Umma's reaction to meeting her long-lost friend made me remember how much they had given up for me. I'd make it up to them by working really hard here.

Umma nudged me and I bowed. "Annyeonghaseyo."

"You must be Lia," the woman said. "You can call me Ms. Shin."

"Uri Lia jal butakhae," Umma said.

"Of course, we'll take excellent care of her," Ms. Shin said as she rubbed Umma's arm. "You have nothing to worry about."

"We appreciate it," said Appa.

Ms. Shin looked at her watch. "We're just about to get started."

During the last couple of minutes, almost all the seats had filled up. Ms. Shin ushered us to our seats, which were in the very first row.

I scanned the area and spotted Joon seated in the back with Ajumma and Ajeossi. I waved my arm in the air, but he was too busy laughing with a group of kids. Leave it to Joon to have already become Mr. Popular. If he hadn't been so focused on passing the IMA exam, I'm sure he would've made a lot of friends at our old school, West Hills. But he hadn't seen a point in making friends with people he'd have to leave behind.

Ms. Shin stood next to the table and spun her hand in the air, and a microphone appeared. "Hello, everyone! We are so excited to welcome our First Years to our International Magic School family. It's going to be an amazing year."

Everyone cheered as Ms. Shin turned around to pick up a uniform bundle, a wallet, and a badge.

"Every First Year student will receive uniforms." She pulled out a shirt from one of the bundles. "Since this is a magic school, we of course need magic clothes."

What? I was going to get magic clothes, too? I clapped along with everyone else.

Ms. Shin held the collar of the shirt with one hand and with her other hand pulled on the center, and a second shirt popped out.

Kids cheered.

"You'll find seven of each item of clothing," she said. "But most importantly, these uniforms are self-cleaning."

Ms. Shin uncapped a black marker from the table and drew a large mark on the white shirt. Then she turned it inside out and waved it gently in the air.

"Shall we see if it's clean now?"

A lot of kids shouted, "Yes!"

When she flipped the shirt back, the stain was gone.

What a genius idea! Too bad I couldn't do this to all my laundry.

Ms. Shin held up a blank card. "This is our newest version of our school badge, which will give you access to all the places you have clearance for, money for meals and snacks, music and video storage, and can store encrypted documents."

Amazing. It was a USB flash drive, security badge, and credit card all rolled into one.

Finally she held up a slim black wallet that looked just like the ones Umma and Appa had. "This is our standard IMA-issued badge holder."

She unzipped it, and the wallet unraveled into a single strand. When Ms. Shin pressed the ends against the badge, they clicked onto it, and she hung it around her neck.

"At school remember to always wear your badge around your neck."

I whispered to Umma, "Does your wallet do that too?"

Umma laughed and squeezed my shoulders. "Of course. But we're not at school or working in an office anymore, so no need for us to use it like a lanyard."

Hmmm. So they'd had this wallet my entire life and I'd never noticed?

This wasn't the best sign for my future career as an agent. Good thing I had tons of time to sharpen my observation skills.

"Let's get started with the initiation ceremony." Ms. Shin talked over the voices in the crowd. "Eugene Yang, please come up."

I turned to see who he was. A tall boy with wavy black hair got up a few rows behind me. Strange that he was here all alone. According to Umma, a parent or at least a guardian usually came to these events. So she had prepped me at home to be polite and gracious to everyone, especially the adults I'd meet.

As soon as he started walking down the aisle, a couple of kids shouted, "Jal saenggyeosseo!"

I held in a giggle, because he didn't seem to appreciate the comments. But I had to agree with everyone: he was really good-looking.

Ms. Shin held out a badge in front of him and motioned for him to place his hand on top of it. "Do you solemnly swear to be courageous, wise, benevolent, and strong?"

"I swear," he said.

"Do you promise to be a good steward of your power?"

"Yes," he answered.

She smiled in approval. "Now close your eyes and try to channel your gi onto the badge. It needs to sense you."

Gi was the energy flowing within you. All living creatures had it. But being able to control and use it was a whole different story.

Eugene did as he was told, and about thirty seconds later the badge dinged and then lit up.

Ms. Shin patted him on the back, and he returned to his seat with the badge around his neck and a uniform bundle.

"Next we have Chloe Shim."

A tall, lanky girl with shoulder-length hair jumped out of her seat and bounded down the aisle. Once she got to the front, she tripped over her shoelaces and crashed into the table. All the clothes and badges toppled onto the ground.

"I'm so sorry," she blubbered, frantically trying to pick everything up.

A few staff members came and helped put everything back on the table.

Ms. Shin pulled Chloe up. "Are you okay?"

"Ne!" she said as she put her hair behind her ears.

Some kids laughed and called out, "Clumsy Chloe!"

I swiveled in my seat and gave them my best evil eye. So rude to be making fun of a person for falling down. She looked flustered but thankfully seemed okay.

Ms. Shin continued with the ceremony, and it took Chloe about a minute to activate the badge using her gi.

"Joon Kim, please come up," said Ms. Shin.

I turned around and called out his name, but my voice was drowned out by his new friends, who chanted, "Jooo-oooon! Jooo-oooon! Jooo-oooon!"

One kid with a shaved head and intense eyes stood up and pumped his fist in the air while shouting Joon's name.

Once Joon got to the front, our eyes met, and he waved at me. I gave him two thumbs-up. He was going to do great. I just knew it.

After answering Ms. Shin's questions, Joon shut his eyes. I squeezed my hands together and waited nervously for the badge to beep.

One, two, three, four, five . . .

Then it lit up.

Daebak. Amazing. Joon's energy must've been really strong for the badge to activate that quickly. Not realizing how silent everyone had gotten, I jumped up and cheered loudly for him. My face turned red as everyone laughed.

Umma tugged at my arm for me to sit back down. Who cared what other people thought? My friend had been the fastest one so far, and I was just really proud of him.

"Next we have Lia Park," Ms. Shin said.

Umma and Appa patted my back. "Hwaiting, Lia ya."

Break a leg. I needed all the luck I could get because I was so nervous.

Since we had sat in the first row, I only had to take a few steps to reach Ms. Shin. In her outstretched hand was a blank badge.

My hand shook, but I placed it firmly on the badge.

"Lia, do you solemnly swear to be courageous, wise, benevolent, and strong?"

"I do." My lips trembled, and I couldn't get my hand to stay still.

Ms. Shin smiled and whispered, "You're doing great."

I stared at Umma and Appa sitting in the front row and breathed in deep. Umma was putting her fingers on her cheeks, reminding me to smile, and Appa was making funny faces. I almost laughed.

"Do you promise to be a good steward of your power?"

"Yes," I said.

"Now try to channel all your gi," she said.

Part of me hoped that I'd beat Joon and activate the

badge faster. I knew this wasn't a race, but I still wanted to win.

I closed my eyes and imagined a tornado of energy spiraling up from deep down inside my abdomen. The gi traveled through my body and down my arms. I could feel it reaching my fingers, tingling all the nerves in my hand.

Almost there.

And then it stopped.

CHAPTER 3

What had just happened? I definitely felt my gi surging and coursing through my body. So how could it just stop when I was so close? It didn't make any sense. I squeezed my eyes tighter together and focused. Just like before, the energy welled up inside me and swooshed up through my arms. I furrowed my brows and concentrated.

Gone.

Ms. Shin whispered, "Is everything okay, Lia?"

"It's not working," I said in a strained voice. "Do you think there's something wrong with my badge?"

"Hmmm. We checked all of these this morning."

Ms. Shin tapped on the badge lightly, and it vibrated. "See? It's working. You're probably just nervous."

Even though something didn't feel right, I couldn't explain it all to Ms. Shin. Especially not right now, in the middle of an initiation ceremony with everyone watching. I'd just have to do the same thing again and trust her that the badge was working.

I closed my eyes and tried again. Maybe because I had used up a lot of my gi already, this time it took longer to get the swirling sensation. Then I coaxed it with my mind to move through my body. It crawled at a snail's space. I scrunched up my forehead and wiped the sweat rolling down my cheeks. Finally my hands tingled, and I felt the energy grow stronger. Using every last ounce of strength, I channeled it to my fingertips. I kept pushing and didn't stop until I heard a ding.

When I opened my eyes, the crowd was silent for a moment before erupting into loud whispers. Some kids covered their mouths with their hands, while others pointed at me.

"I thought she was supposed to be powerful," someone said.

"Not impressed at all," said another voice.

"I bet my baby brother could do it faster than that."

My face turned bright red. This was so frustrating, and I wished I could shout and tell everyone that my badge was broken. But that would just be embarrassing.

Ms. Shin patted my back. "The important thing is that you activated it."

"How long did it take?" I guessed maybe a minute? A little under two?

She paused and then whispered, "Five minutes."

My eyes almost bulged out of my face. Did she say five entire minutes? That couldn't be right. It didn't feel like I'd been standing there for five minutes. And it was also completely unfair, because something had been wrong with my badge, and I had depleted my energy the second time around.

I walked back to my seat, and Umma hugged me. "I'm proud of you for giving it your best shot and not quitting."

That should've made me feel better, but it didn't.

After the initiation ceremony, everyone headed to the welcome dinner, which was also on the lawn. Because it was buffet style, we grabbed our food first and then joined Ajumma, Ajeossi, and Joon, who were just about to sit down.

"Annyeonghaseyo." I bowed to them.

"Oneul sugohasseo," Ajumma said.

"Thank you." I knew she was just being kind, because I hadn't done a great job today at all.

All my frustrations melted away when I saw my friend. What had happened at the ceremony was just a tiny blip in what was obviously going to be an amazing year. So what if people were talking about me? I'd prove them wrong, and they'd see that it really wasn't me but a malfunctioning badge.

"Joon," I said, giving him a big hug. "Can you believe it? We're finally here!"

He grinned and put his arm around my shoulders. "It's so much better than we imagined."

I set my plate down and scooted my chair closer to his so that we could talk without the parents listening.

"What top secret info do you have?" Joon asked in a hushed voice.

I was so glad he understood our secret signal. We'd only been practicing it forever, since we were kids. That was why we'd make the best duo ever. We were on our way to becoming legendary agents!

I stuffed a chopstickful of japchae—stir-fried noodles and vegetables—into my mouth.

The boy with the shaved head walked by and gave

Joon a high five. "We're sitting over there," he said, pointing to a table near the food. "Want to join?"

"Next time," Joon said. "This is my friend Lia."

"Victor," he said. "See you at the house, then."

Joon nodded and waved as Victor walked away.

"Look at you," I said, patting his back. "Such a social butterfly."

He flapped his arms up and down. "Are you getting jealous?"

"Nope," I said. "Because I'm still your best friend, and your friends can be my friends too."

We tapped our badges together and shouted, "Team super agents!"

"You were amazing today," I said. "I can't believe you beat out everyone else."

He shrugged and looked a little flustered. "Thanks, but it wasn't a competition. I wasn't expecting it to light up so fast either."

True. It wasn't a race, but he had still impressed all the other First Years. I was sure of it. Whether he wanted to admit it or not, there was an unspoken respect given to those who performed well today.

"What happened up there?" Joon whispered. "I know you, and you could've made way better time than that."

I leaned in and lowered my voice. "Right before my gi reached the badge, it just stopped. I think something was blocking my gi from activating it."

"Huh," he said. "Did you stop concentrating?"

"Of course not," I said. "Why would I do that?" He knew how competitive I got sometimes.

"Then how come it didn't work?" he asked.

"Because." I sighed with frustration. "I got a faulty badge."

Clearly this was the reason. No doubt in my mind, because I knew what I'd felt.

Joon used his chopsticks to split the kimchi into smaller, bite-friendly pieces. "But we all saw her check the badge," he said. "And yours worked eventually."

"What? You don't believe me?"

"Lia, you're my best friend," he said. "Of course I believe you, but it's strange that no one else had that problem."

I guess it was. But it would have been great if he'd been on my side, even if I was wrong. At least for a little moment, before trying to reason things out. After everything we'd gone through last year, Joon of all people should have known that when it involved IMA, some things couldn't really be explained rationally, and as agents in training, we needed to trust our instincts.

"It just didn't feel right," I said. "That's all."

He ate a piece of LA galbi and wiped his mouth with his napkin. "Not everything's a conspiracy, and not everyone is out to get you."

I gulped down my water. "So what are you trying to say?" He should've just said what he thought instead of tiptoeing around it.

"It could just be you, Lia."

Ouch. Even though I knew that was what he was trying to get at, it was still really hurtful to hear and really not how I had pictured this chat with Joon going. "But I swear it wasn't me."

He must've known he'd said the wrong thing, because he quickly added, "You could've been too excited or distracted, or a million other different things."

It was so frustrating that I couldn't prove to anyone what I'd felt inside my body, how I'd felt something had gone wrong. All everyone saw and judged me by were the results. Eventually I'd been able to activate the card, but I knew in my gut that something had felt off in that moment.

"Well, I really think there was something wrong with my badge."

"Okay," he said. "I think that's a possibility too."

We ate the rest of the meal in silence.

Once dinner was over, Ms. Shin stood in front of the buffet table. "Thank you, parents, for trusting us with your children. It's now time to say your goodbyes."

Four older students held up signs of the blue dragon, the white tiger, the red-vermilion bird, and the black turtle.

"When you are done," Ms. Shin said, "please find the symbol for your house."

Umma and Appa hugged me tight. I was going to miss these group hugs.

"You're going to love it here," Appa said.

Umma wiped a tear from her face. "Whenever you need us, we're just a phone call away."

"Or even a text," Appa joked.

"Saranghae, Lia ya," Umma said, kissing my cheek.

"I love you too." I waved as I walked toward the line with the blue dragon sign. I must've been the last one there, because no one else rushed to stand behind me.

The girl holding the blue dragon sign was short, with long, curly hair and large sunglasses propped up on her head. She pointed to each person and counted the First Years in her line.

"Twelve," she said. "Now that we're all here, my name is Katie, and I'm the house president this year."

We walked past the academic building, which was pretty massive, with three floors.

"This is where all your classes will be," she said.

Then she opened a gate, and we crossed a large field. It was at least twice the size of the one we had back at West Hills. But other than that, it didn't look or feel any different.

"This is where we will have a lot of magic sparring battles, competitions, and sports," Katie said.

"What kind of sports?" asked a girl with white headphones that had purple trim.

"We have our own versions of certain sports, like soccer, dodgeball, and basketball," Katie said.

On the other side of the field were rows of bleachers. That must have been where we would get to sit and watch these games. I couldn't wait to find out how to play.

Katie gestured to a giant blue dragon statue in front of a subway station. "This is our very own hyperloop train station. Each dorm and academic building has a stop."

She continued to talk as we walked. "The four houses—House of Wisdom, House of Courage, House of Strength, and House of Benevolence—are located in the north, south, west, and east corners of the campus."

It made sense that the placement of the houses matched the cardinal direction that they represented.

Since I was in the House of Benevolence, we were probably headed to the eastern part of the school.

Katie continued, "Each house also has a mythological guardian animal—black turtle in the north, red-vermilion bird in the south, white tiger in the west, and blue dragon in the east."

Soon we were standing in front of a building that looked like a giant dragon with a jewel in its opened mouth. I got goose bumps just looking at it. Unlike the one I'd seen earlier, this house was longer than it was tall.

Katie took out her badge and slid it inside a groove in the middle of the jewel. Then the jewel split in half and opened up.

Oh my goodness. This was the coolest house ever. Walking in through the dragon's mouth made me feel invincible, like I was the most courageous person, walking straight into the belly of a powerful beast.

"Welcome home, everyone," Katie said.

Dragon-shaped lamps on the walls and large chandeliers made entirely of dangling jewels lit up the room. Velvety blue sofas sat in the middle of the room, while built-in bookshelves lined the walls.

"This is our living room, where we hang out after school," she said.

Everything was so sparkly and luxurious. Was this really my new life?

Katie took a tablet from her bag and tapped it. "Oh good, your luggage has been delivered to your rooms."

I was so relieved that mine was already here, safe and sound.

"Your room assignments should be on your badges now," she said. "Please check."

Mine showed my picture and three lines below it, which read *Lia Park, First Year, House of Benevolence.* As I stared at it, a fourth line appeared: *Room 35.*

"All First Years will have roommates," Katie said. "This is to help each other get adjusted."

I wondered who my roommate was going to be. Whoever it was, I really hoped we'd get along.

She stood in front of two elevators with the numbers one and two painted on the doors. "These lead to the dorms," Katie continued. "If you're in rooms one to thirty-three, take elevator one. And if you're in rooms thirty-four to sixty-six, take elevator two."

I waited in front of elevator number two, while everyone else moved to the other one. Except for one person.

"I guess we're roommates," I said, and walked into the open elevator. "I'm Lia."

The girl with the headphones nodded and said, "I'm Rae."

I was surprised she'd heard me. Maybe she wasn't really listening to anything.

Thankfully, it was a really short ride, and I didn't have to figure out something else to say to her. We walked down the hall and passed by a communal bathroom, a living room, and a kitchen, and finally came to room 35.

Off to the right side of the door were two metal boxes placed on top of each other. The top one had *R. Kim* stenciled on, and the bottom read *L. Park.*

I tugged on the latch of my box, but it wouldn't open, which made me even more curious to see what was inside.

Rae placed the badge hanging around her neck against the front of her box, and it clicked open.

So, Ms. Shin really wasn't joking about the badges giving us access to pretty much everything at school.

Rae found a letter inside and moved to the left to read it.

I quickly sat down and tapped my badge against my box. Once I heard the click, I flipped it open. It just looked like the inside of a box. Nothing extraordinary.

There was a small open container of trapezoid-shaped tags with an elastic band attached, two black markers, and a folded letter.

The letter read:

Welcome from International Magic School's mail services.

All mail will be delivered to your individual mailbox.

To send mail, follow the instructions below:

1. Write full name and house of student on tag using the marker provided (they are magical).

2. Attach securely to letter or package.

3. Leave in box and close.

4. Should disappear within five minutes. If it doesn't, contact mail services.

Rae pressed her badge against a keypad on the wall, and the door to our room opened on its own.

Both sides of the room looked identical, each with a bed, a desk, and a dresser. On each bed was a copy of the

International Magic School student handbook. The only thing we shared was the mirrored closet next to the door. Our suitcases stood in the middle of the room.

"So which side do you want?" I shouted, in case she actually had music on.

"You don't have to yell. I can hear you just fine," Rae said, and plopped down on the bed facing the door. "I can't sleep facing a mirror."

"Sorry, I thought you wouldn't be able to hear with those on," I said.

She smirked and tapped her headphones. "This is so I won't have to deal with small talk with people."

I dragged my suitcase to my side of the room. "Totally fooled me." She pulled the headphones off and handed them to me. I put them on my ears, and just as I had started to suspect, there was no sound at all.

"See," she said, putting them back on. "The perfect excuse to avoid talkers."

Then she pointed to the mirror. "You know the saying, right?"

I had no idea what she was talking about. "Not sure."

"That your soul could be stolen if you sleep in front of one," she explained.

"Uh, thanks for sharing." I had not heard that before,

but it definitely made me want to find a sheet to cover up the mirror. I wasn't very superstitious, but once I heard about things like this, why tempt fate?

"Oh, and you should make sure to push your chair all the way in before you sleep."

Did I really want to know why? But I couldn't help myself. "And why is that?"

"Have you been living under a rock? I can't believe you don't know this stuff," she said in an exasperated voice. "Because it's like an invitation for a ghost to come and sit and watch you."

I pushed my chair in firmly under the desk. "Why would they want to watch me?"

"To gawi nulreo you while you are sleeping," she said matter-of-factly.

I'd never experienced it myself, but apparently, it was this feeling of being crushed by a ghost or evil spirit when they pressed down on your body while you were sleeping.

Maybe Rae liked spooky stories. I took out my book of Korean folktales, which I'd had since I was little, and flipped through the pages. "Have you heard about the gumiho?"

She perked up and took off her headphones. "Of course," she said. "The nine-tailed fox that eats the livers of men so she can someday turn into a woman."

"How about the dalgyal gwishin?"

"An egg ghost?" she asked. "Never heard of it."

I showed her the picture in my book of a faceless ghost. It literally had an egg-shaped head with no facial features whatsoever. "These ghosts just like to hunt people for fun."

"Oh my gosh, Lia," she groaned. "Stop telling me such scary stories."

"Don't worry," I said as I closed the book. "They only live in forests." As soon as I said that, I realized that the entire campus was surrounded by trees and there was a giant mountain behind the school.

"That does not make me feel better," she said.

"My mom said that this school has top-notch security," I said. "No one and nothing can get in or out."

"Nothing's a hundred percent," she said, and turned her back to me.

I still saw it as a win that she had actually taken off her headphones to talk to me. That meant I was interesting. I'd have to research more on ghosts so I could chat with her about them.

When I came back from washing up, Rae had already turned off the lights. I fumbled my way across the room, pulled on my sleep mask, and climbed into bed.

Suddenly the light flipped on, and I felt someone hovering over me.

I startled, pulled off my sleep mask, and squinted from the bright light.

"Wait," said Rae. "You're Lia Park as in the girl who used the jewel's powers?"

Before I could answer, Rae gasped and pointed at me. "There it is, the white hair."

I frantically patted my hair and realized my hair was down. Darn it. It was a habit to untie my hair before bed.

She continued to shoot questions at me. "So are you soulless now? What did it feel like?"

This was exactly why I'd hidden the white streak today. I knew I wouldn't be able to conceal it forever, since everyone would be living together, but I hadn't expected someone to find out so soon.

"Did destroying the jewel take away your power?" She took a deep breath and then continued, "Maybe that's why the badge didn't work for you."

I didn't have any answers to her questions and didn't like how it felt like an interrogation.

"Good night, Rae," I snapped.

I tugged the sleep mask back over my eyes.

CHAPTER 4

Hwarang training wouldn't start until the second week of school. But I got up early and left before Rae woke up. I knew I wouldn't be able to avoid all her questions forever, since unfortunately, she was my roommate, and I was stuck with her for an entire year. But I didn't want to deal with it this morning. I patted the top of my head to make sure my bobby pins were in place. Nothing could ruin my first amazing, fantastic day at school.

My first class of the day was Korean history. By the time I got to class, Joon was already there. I slid into the desk next to him.

"Thanks for saving my spot," I said.

He took his backpack off my desk and smiled. "Anytime."

In front of me sat someone wearing the exact same jacket Umma had, except this one had orange stripes down the side.

I tapped his shoulder. "Are you a Hwarang?"

He turned around, and I was surprised to see that it was Eugene.

"Yeah," he said. "This was my dad's."

"I wish I'd worn my mom's today," I said. I'd left Umma's jacket in the suitcase because I didn't want to draw attention to myself. But after seeing Eugene wearing his dad's, I kind of regretted it.

A short man with big black sunglasses and a hat walked into the classroom, followed by a group of kids wearing costumes.

"My name is Mr. Yu," he said. "Please get into your seats."

Once we settled down, a kid with a long white beard, wearing a white robe with a golden crown, moved next to him.

"It's tradition for the Second Years to welcome the First Years with a short play on the foundation mythology," said Mr. Yu. "This is also an opportunity to showcase your unique powers."

Everyone clapped and cheered. I couldn't wait to see it. Especially the magic.

"I am Hwanin, the creator god," bellowed the kid. He reached his hands powerfully up, and thunderbolts shot out of his hands.

Then another kid, dressed in a blue robe with a gold band around his head, entered the room. "Abeoji," he said. "I wish to live on earth."

"Hwanung, my son," said Hwanin. "If you must go, take our subjects."

The rest of the kids, in intricate hairstyles and dressed in black robes, entered. "We are the three thousand subjects here to serve you." They bowed, but one kid's hairpiece fell off.

Everyone laughed, but I said loudly, "Gwaenchana!"

I wanted him to know it was okay so that he could keep going.

The kid put his wig back on and mouthed, "Thank you!"

One by one, the kids showed off their skills. The first student floated about six inches off the floor. Another became invisible for a few seconds, while the next couple of kids took out weights from under their robes and held them up using just their index fingers.

A few others just smiled and stood in place. My guess was that they probably had magic that couldn't really be seen, not as flashy but just as powerful.

"I will also give you three heavenly heirlooms," said Hwanin.

He plucked at the air in front of him, and a flat, circular object appeared.

Everyone in the audience clapped.

"This mirror will reflect the beauty of nature."

Then he pulled another object out of thin air. It looked like a multi-pointed star, except the points had round balls attached to them. "A rattle holding the sounds of heaven and earth."

For the last object, he sliced the air with his hands, and a dagger appeared before him. "The dagger of justice."

Hwanin handed the heavenly heirlooms to Hwanung. "Together they will create fire and light for the human realm. And the dagger will bring order."

Hwanung knelt down before Hwanin. "Thank you, Father," he said. "I will use them to rule well."

Just then a bear and a tiger bounded into the room.

Everyone gasped. No doubt in my mind that they were shape-shifters.

"We want to be human," said the bear.

Hwanung gave the bear and tiger mugwort and an armful of garlic. "Eat this and stay out of the sun for one hundred days."

The tiger ate a little bit and threw it onto the floor. He leaped out of the room.

As soon as the bear had eaten everything, gold sparkles enveloped the bear, and it transformed into a woman.

Hwanung held the woman's hand. "Will you marry me?"

They walked out of the room together and returned with another boy dressed in gold-and-blue robes. The boy held the heavenly heirlooms up to the ceiling. "I am Dangun, the founder of Gojoseon, the first kingdom of Korea."

Everyone cheered and clapped.

All of a sudden, a girl dressed in a yellow hanbok with rainbow-colored sleeves took the heavenly heirlooms from Dangun and threw them back into the air. They flickered and then disappeared.

"The heavenly heirlooms proved too powerful for any one human to possess, so they were split up and hidden away forever, never to be seen again," said the girl in the yellow hanbok.

The tiger came back into the room and shape-shifted

into a boy. He joined the rest of his classmates, who were standing in a line, and everyone bowed. We all stood up and cheered. They were pretty good, and I loved the brilliant costumes and the magic.

"Thank you, Second Years," Mr. Yu said.

The kids waved and then exited the room.

Unfortunately, the rest of his class was not quite as interesting. Mr. Yu's voice was too soothing and calm. And even though some of the stuff was kind of cool, how could anything he said top the play we had just seen?

My Korean language class and math class were pretty uneventful. But I was most excited for my very first Spells class, which was right after lunch. Technically, I'd never taken a class in spellmaking because I had uncovered my power accidentally. Learning from Umma's book didn't really count, because I wasn't sure if I was doing it right half the time.

A petite lady dressed in a billowy skirt with a floral pattern and a white top entered the classroom. "Good afternoon, everyone," she said. "My name is Ms. Cho."

"Good afternoon," we said in unison.

"With a show of hands," she said, "how many spell casters do we have?"

About three quarters of the class raised their hands.

"Everyone with their hands down should be spell-makers," she said. "Or you are in the wrong class."

I laughed nervously. It felt good to be with people just like me. Victor sat a few seats behind me. Finally, a familiar face. I waved, and he awkwardly smiled back.

"Today we will practice basic skills." She placed her coffee mug in front of her and commanded, "Idong." Instantly it flew into her hands.

Whew. For a moment I was worried she might've requested a different beginner-level spell I hadn't mastered yet. Thank goodness this was one of the first ones I ever learned through Umma's journal.

"Form a line next to my desk," she said. "We will go one by one."

I got up and walked as fast as I could to get to the start of the line, but I was too slow. There were already seven people ahead of me. That was okay. It gave me time to practice in my head. I chanted the word and imagined it over and over.

The line moved quickly as everyone completed their spell in less than a few seconds. Finally it was my turn. I stood in front of the cup and chanted, "Idong!"

It didn't budge.

Victor snickered and said, "She's a joke."

Ms. Cho stared him down and spoke in an even-toned voice, which made her sound even scarier. "Victor, I will not tolerate that kind of behavior in my classroom."

"Sorry," he said, and sat down in the seat right in front of the desk.

She turned to me and said, "Lia, focus and try again."

I pictured the cup in my hands and chanted, "Idong."

The cup wiggled a little and then stopped. I could feel Victor's eye boring into me and tried my best to ignore him.

"Lia," said Ms. Cho. "I need you to command it like you believe it."

I'd been doing that already, but I nodded. "Idong," I said in a firm voice.

This time, the cup smashed into the wall and shattered on the floor.

Kids screamed and moved away from the broken shards, while others got completely splashed with coffee. I wiped coffee off my arm. Thankfully, the liquid wasn't hot.

"That's enough for today," Ms. Cho said. "Please get cleaned up."

Then she turned to me and said, "Lia, you need to keep practicing. These are very basic skills."

I held back the tears in my eyes and nodded. What was Victor's problem anyway? The way he'd been staring at me had completely thrown me off. I couldn't think of anything I'd done to make him dislike me. I mean, school had just started, and I'd never even talked to him before. There was no way I could defend myself and make Ms. Cho believe that I had mastered this spell, without sounding like I was making up another excuse for why I couldn't perform.

After changing, I headed into my final class for the day, Tinkergets. It was officially called Tinker Gadgets, but all the kids shortened the name by combining the two words. Only catch, *gets* was pronounced as *jets* like in *gadgets*.

Even before I entered the classroom, I could hear Victor's booming voice.

Inside, there were six round tables, three in each row, with four chairs to a table. I found an empty table as far away as possible from him and sat down.

The classroom filled up pretty quickly, but nobody joined my table.

Then Eugene walked in and sat down across from me.

Whew. At least we were both Hwarang. That must mean something.

Rae waved at me and sat down at a different table. I was slightly relieved that she didn't join our table.

I heard Victor shout, "Joon, my friend!" His table was full, so he nudged the kid sitting next to him to get up so that Joon could sit there.

"It's okay," Joon said to the kid who had gotten up.

I waved Joon over, and he sat down next to me.

"Are you close to Victor?" I demanded.

"Oh, Vic?" Joon said. "You met him at dinner, remember? He's a good person."

I couldn't believe Joon actually thought Victor was a nice guy. He was super rude and just plain old mean. Not a single nice bone in his body. I mean, that stare he'd given me during Spells class was ice-cold.

"Has he said anything about me?" I asked. "Because I don't think he likes me very much."

"No," Joon said. "Not everything is about you, Lia."

Again, why was he taking it the wrong way? That wasn't how I'd meant it at all. "I just got a bad feeling about him in Spells class today."

"I'm sure if you really got to know him, you'd think he

was really funny and had a lot of cool stories," Joon said in a defensive tone.

I highly doubted that, but I didn't really want to argue with him about it. "Maybe," I said.

"I don't think he's a very nice guy, actually," Eugene chimed in.

"Who asked you?" Joon said.

Thankfully, just at the right time Chloe sat down at our table. I remembered her name because everyone had made fun of her at the initiation ceremony, and I just felt for her.

She pulled out her tablet, which had a giant picture of Jay One on the back.

"Oh my gosh," I shouted. "I love Jay One."

Chloe stretched out her arms and stuck up only her index fingers, forming a little V.

I laughed and did the same with my hands. This was the jjin paen symbol. Only real true fans knew it, and we called ourselves Jay Twos because we would always be there to support our oppas.

"I'm so happy you love them too," Chloe said.

I was so excited that I didn't even see the teacher walk in. When I looked up, he had written his name in big letters on the board behind him. *Mr. Koo.*

"The people you are sitting with will be your team-mates all year," he said. "Please come up with a team name."

"Any thoughts?" I asked our table. "Should we just throw some names out there?"

"How about something like 'Marvelous'?" Chloe said.

"The Power Quartet," I said.

"Infinity," Eugene said.

"Or 'Dream Team,'" Joon added.

None of those felt right.

"How about we come up with some words that start with the first letters of our names?" I suggested.

"Good idea," Chloe said. She started typing on her tablet.

"I'll go first," Joon said. "I have *Lion, Jester, Endless, Craft*."

"*Limitless, Journey, Enjoyable, Consistent,*" Eugene said.

"*Legendary, Justice, Ecstatic, Crystals,*" said Chloe.

"*Lovable, Joy, Elevated, Crane,*" I said.

All those words sounded pretty good. I ran different combinations in my head until it just hit me. "I got it," I said. "Legendary Journey Elevated Craft."

"That's actually pretty good," Eugene said.

Joon nodded. "And it has meaning, because I'm sure that's what we all want, right?"

"Yeah," Chloe said. "I'd love to have a legendary journey and elevate my craft."

I repeated the letters in my head faster and faster. "El-jeck."

"Oh!" Chloe shouted. "*Jeck* sounds kind of like *check*."

"That's a stretch," Joon said.

"Well, if you pronounce it Korean style like *jeh-keu*, it sounds like Korean style *che-keu*," I explained.

Eugene laughed. "It does sound similar."

Joon groaned. "Fine, I'm on the corniest team."

I ignored his comment. "So we have *check*."

"In slow-motion, it's *el-leu*," Eugene said.

"Not sure there's a word that sounds like that," Chloe said.

I went over different ways to say *l* really fast and slow in my head to come up with a word. The closest one I got was obviously a very forced match. But I'd rather share my opinion than not contribute at all because it sounded funny.

"How about it?" I said hesitantly.

"Hmmm," Eugene said. "That doesn't really sound like *l* at all, but I don't have a better word."

"Actually, that's a brilliant play on words," Joon said. "We all need to take a breather."

"I get it," Chloe said. "When things get tough, take a deep breath and carry on."

I beamed and stuck my hand out in the middle of the table. "Team Air Check."

One by one, everyone piled their hands on top of each other. Then we shouted, "Air Check!"

Mr. Koo clapped his hands. "Looks like table three is the first one ready."

He pointed to six large bins on the table at the front of the classroom. "Once you're done coming up with your table's team name, take one bin. All we're going to do today is mix different concoctions so we can use them for future classes."

Joon and Chloe went to the front and carried a bin over to our table.

"Spend some time getting to know each other," Mr. Koo said. "Figure out how you can utilize each of your strengths."

"I think we should know each other's power," I said. "I'm a spellmaker."

Chloe and Joon placed the materials and a piece of paper with instructions in the center of the table.

"I've never met a spellmaker before," Chloe said. "They're kind of rare, aren't they?"

Joon nodded. "Yeah, I only have one other friend who's a spellmaker."

Ugh, was he talking about Victor? I couldn't believe Joon was calling Victor his friend again after everything I'd just told him.

"I have healing powers," Joon said.

"That's cool," Eugene said. "So we could be a little reckless, and you'd patch us up?"

Joon looked down and said, "Sorry, I can only heal myself."

"Guess it's the infirmary for us, then," Eugene said. "I can stop time."

"That's so neat!" I said. "For how long?"

"I'm at five seconds these days," Eugene said.

"Is there really anything you can do in just five seconds?" Joon asked.

Eugene didn't even flinch and answered in a calm voice, "Actually depends on how quick you are, but I get a lot done."

"We should test it out next time and see how many things we can do," Chloe said.

"And what's your power?" Joon asked her.

She pulled an assortment of black microchips from her bag. "I can talk to machines and program these."

"Wow," I said. "Our team is going to rock it."

This was Tinkergets class after all, which meant we'd

be inventing and making cool gadgets, and we happened to have the resident tech genius on our team.

Following the instruction sheet, Chloe poured a red liquid into jar number one. Then I added two drops of a clear substance, using a pipette. We left the lid open and waited for the mixture to settle.

Joon and Eugene worked separately on their own concoctions.

"How many more do we have to make?" I asked.

Chloe looked at the instructions. "It says three more."

Using a funnel, I poured a metallic powder into a second jar. Then Chloe gently dropped in three sprigs of rosemary. The powder began to circle around the leaves and disintegrated them all within a few seconds. The bits of green mixed with the metallic powder and seemed to balance it out.

From the corner of my eye, I spotted Victor staring at me and moving his lips. I frowned and looked over at Joon, who was so focused on making his concoction that he totally missed seeing how strangely Victor was acting toward me.

For the last mixture, Chloe used tongs to grab some pointy crystals and placed them gently into the jar. I poured in a blue liquid and stopped once it reached the halfway mark. The crystals began to bounce around, and some even popped up over the liquid before dropping back in.

"Is it supposed to be doing that?" I asked Mr. Koo.

"Yes, it should stop soon," he said.

But the crystals grew more aggressive and clinked against the jar. The sound grew louder and louder. There was a crack, and then the jar exploded.

I shrieked and covered my face, but Eugene swooped in and shielded me by putting his back to the explosion.

The Hwarang jacket was splattered with the mixture, but all the glass pieces just slid off. There must've been some special magic on those jackets.

"Thank you," I blubbered. "You saved me."

"We Hwarangs have to look out for each other, right?" he said.

"Are you okay?" Joon said. He picked a piece of glass from my hair.

I nodded. Thankfully, I had no cuts or bruises because of how fast Eugene had been.

"Was that Lia again?" Victor called out from his seat across the room.

I shot him a dirty look.

He just smirked and said, "She's cursed, you know."

CHAPTER 5

The first four weeks of school had been a disaster. Victor's offhand comment started a whole bunch of rumors. I heard everything, but the worst one, the one that bothered me the most, was that I was a nakhasan, which literally translated to *parachute*. It meant that I had only gotten into IMS because of connections, like my parents being legendary agents and good friends with the headmaster, even though I had no real skill or talent of my own.

My extremely unpredictable spellmaking power only added fuel to the rumors. It was as if I had lost all control over whether my powers would appear or not.

I hoped our class's first field trip would help patch things up between me and Joon.

Ganghwado was a small island right next to Incheon, where the international airport was located. Today we were going to Chamseongdan located on Ganghwado Island to celebrate Gaecheonjeol, which literally meant *the day heaven opened*. October 3 was a national holiday, commemorating the day that Dangun founded Korea's first kingdom, Gojoseon, in 2333 BC.

Only select members of the magic community were allowed to attend the special ceremonial performance at Chamseongdan, where Dangun was said to have offered sacrifices to the heavens. And each year, the new class of incoming First Year students was also invited. Everyone else had the day off.

To be honest, I had no idea what to expect on our first-ever field trip. Of course, I had gone on field trips back in California to the zoo or to the park, all by bus.

But this was no ordinary field trip or school.

Because everything here was magical.

The First Years had all gathered in the transportation room at the school. Rows and rows of giant square glass lanterns filled up the room, which was as big as five basketball courts. In the IMS student handbook, which

I'd practically memorized by now, the facilities section included three whole pages on the transportation room.

During the Joseon dynasty, glass lanterns that hung in the royal palace had floral decorations painted on each side. The ones in this room had paintings of the four guardians: the blue dragon, the red-vermilion bird, the white tiger, and the black turtle. Each lantern was a type of one-way portal into a specific tourist area or neighborhood in Korea. The portals were then immediately turned off to prevent intruders.

The last line of the transportation-room-related pages was a warning written in all caps that read *CAN BE ACTI-VATED ONLY BY TEACHERS*. I didn't have a photographic memory like Appa, but some things were really hard to forget, and when I'd accidentally grazed my hand over that particular sentence, a loud, booming voice had shouted, "Do not tamper with the portals."

As we stood in line, waiting our turn to enter the lantern portal to Ganghwado, Chloe tapped my shoulder and said, "What do you think it'll feel like?"

Hmmm. Good question. I'd only used the transportation coin before. Maybe this would be similar? "All I remember from the transportation coin was a burst of light and feeling warm," I said.

"Oh, that's right," she said. "Probably like the personal coins our parents have."

Not everyone had those devices, though. They were given to top agents and high-ranking officials. I wasn't sure what exactly Chloe's parents did, but rumors were that her family was pretty well connected.

"Do you think there's a chair in there? Or maybe we'll have to stand the whole time?" Chloe took a short breath and then added, "How do you think it'll work?"

I giggled. "You and your million-and-one questions."

Chloe was really into figuring out exactly how things worked, except sometimes with magic, it wasn't possible. Because, well, that was why it was magic.

"Next," called out Ms. Shin.

"I know—maybe it has to do with molecules and atoms," said Chloe. "I hope you make it out in one piece."

I climbed up the three steps to the portal's door and pulled at the ring-shaped handle. "See you on the other side."

Even though these lantern portals were made of glass, they were not see-through at all. The glass on the portal was pretty thick, and there was definitely magical glaze on it, because I couldn't see through it, and kids on the outside couldn't see what was going on inside. It was like the one-way glass in the interrogation rooms that I saw in movies, except it was zero-way glass.

Inside, where the candle would've been, was a large, round white pouf. On the wall across from the door was a sign that read *Sit down*. To my right was a large rectangular button that read *Push me*.

I pressed the button and sat down.

This was it. My moment of truth.

I waited for something magical to happen.

Absolutely nothing.

No sound, no bright lights or temperature changes.

The button didn't even change colors, so I couldn't tell whether it was working.

Oh no. Maybe it was broken.

Ms. Shin would know how to fix it.

I stood back up and yanked the door open, but instead of seeing Chloe waiting in line, I saw blackness. It was completely pitch-dark.

The air was so heavy, I could barely breathe.

I slammed the door shut and frantically pressed the button.

It turned yellow.

Whoosh.

The lantern shook violently. I gripped the handle on

the inside of the door. But I couldn't keep my balance. I collapsed onto the floor, and everything went black.

Something tickled my nose, and a pungent smell overpowered my senses. I jolted up. The last thing I remembered was falling in the lantern. When I opened my eyes, I was sitting in what looked to be an office, with Ms. Shin hovering above me. I rubbed my head and almost yelled in shock when I felt a giant bump on my forehead.

"What happened?" She handed me an ice pack and motioned for me to put it on my head. "Were you standing?"

"Sort of, but—"

She cut me off and said in a very stern voice, "Lia, you need to learn how to follow instructions."

"I can explain," I said.

"There was clearly a pouf and a sign that said to sit down," she said. "You were not sitting, because if you had been, you wouldn't have fallen."

"But I was at first!" I retorted.

"Young lady, do not take that tone of voice with me."

"But—"

She got up and opened the door of the office. "I'm going to have to write you up."

My head spun as I stood. "For what?"

"Blatant disregard for rules," she said. "The rules are here for our safety."

"But it's not my fault," I blurted out. "The portal wasn't working, and I saw just darkness."

Her face froze for a second. "What do you mean *darkness*?"

Finally she was listening to me. "The button didn't work, so I opened the door."

Ms. Shin pulled out her tablet and began to type on it.

"It was just black outside." I shuddered, thinking about it.

She furrowed her eyebrows together. "But what did it feel like? Smell like?"

I didn't have the words to describe it. "Icky. And just a lot of heaviness."

She grimaced and was about to ask me something but stopped herself. "That's not possible."

"I swear it happened!"

Ms. Shin regained her composure and spoke in a soft voice. "I'm sure it was just a temporary technical malfunction. You made it to Ganghwado safe and sound, right?"

I guessed so.

But somehow she didn't sound that convinced herself.

Ms. Shin closed her tablet and ushered me out the door to where all the other kids were waiting in front of a row of buses. For a moment, I forgot about the lantern and marveled at the fact that we had made it to the Ganghwado bus terminal.

I was itching to tell my friends all about what had just happened to me. I scanned the crowd for them and spotted Joon, Chloe, and Eugene rushing over toward me.

"Are you okay?" Chloe asked as she looked me up and down.

"What happened?" Joon asked.

Eugene checked his watch. "You were missing for almost ten minutes." He put his hands up in the air and said, "It wasn't me. You know I can't stop time for that long."

"I know," I reassured him. Using his power also depleted his energy, and he seemed fine right now.

"On the bus, now," Ms. Shin commanded.

I climbed onto the bus and slid into an empty seat. Joon sat down next to me, while Eugene and Chloe plopped down in front of us.

"We can hear you from here, so just keep talking," Eugene whispered really loudly.

I smooshed my face against the back of the seat in front of us and filled everyone in on what had happened.

Even though it had happened so fast, I was 110 percent sure I hadn't imagined the eerie sensations.

"Maybe it was a malfunction," Chloe said. "Like a computer error but with magic."

Even though Chloe was the tech genius, for once her explanation wasn't too logical. I looked over at Joon, who was frowning and shaking his head.

"Mal do andwae," muttered Eugene.

"Yeah, that doesn't make sense to me either," I said. "Even though Ms. Shin said the same thing you did, Chloe."

"Then maybe it was an in-between space," Chloe said. "And you opened the door too early."

Maybe that was what had happened.

"That's so cool," said Eugene. "It's like when I stop time, you were also able to see the transition phase."

"What are you talking about, Eugene?" Joon crossed his arms and leaned back against his seat. This was his thinking pose.

Eugene peeked his face between the seats. "Well, do you have a better idea?"

"I think the machine wasn't completely powered up," Joon said.

"That theory works for me," said Chloe.

"I can live with that," I chimed in.

But this felt eerily like déjà vu, a repeat of when my badge hadn't lit up during the initiation ceremony, and all the times since I'd gotten to school when my magic would just decide not to show up.

"Maybe I am cursed after all," I said half jokingly.

"Seriously, Lia? This again?" Eugene said in a frustrated voice.

Chloe popped her head over the seat. "You are so not cursed. Don't listen to those haters. Right, Joon?"

We all looked at Joon, who turned a little red and mumbled, "Of course you're not."

Part of me wanted to believe them, but something had to be wrong with me for all these things to happen only to me.

It wasn't normal.

"Team Air Check forever," I said. "And besides, none of the teachers seem worried about it." I mean, if this was something that was super dangerous, I was sure we would've all been sent back to school, where there were a million safety protocols in place.

Eugene laughed and said, "Great. We all agree on something for once."

The bus took a sharp turn, and everyone cried out in

surprise, which was then followed by nervous laughter. We had turned off the main road and were driving on a completely unpaved gravel path surrounded by tall trees.

Ms. Shin stood up and held on to a pole at the front of the bus. "Make sure your seat belts are buckled really tightly. It's going to be a bumpy ride from here on out."

I tugged at the strap on my seat belt and pulled it until it wouldn't budge anymore.

The bus took us deeper into the forest. Leaves and branches scraped my window, and I instinctively ducked my head. I hoped no one saw that. It was an odd feeling to stay still when things kept thudding on our windows. As the bus drew to a stop, I stared in awe at the leaves on the trees.

"Do you see that?" I jammed my finger against the window.

Joon peered over. "That we're completely surrounded by an army of trees?"

"It's in the details, remember?"

He squinted. "Now I see it."

Every single leaf on the trees was tilted upward, as if there was an enormous fan on the ground blowing up into the air.

According to Korean mythology, this was a sacred site.

So every year on this date, some aspects of physics didn't apply. This must've been one of those exceptions.

Ms. Shin opened the door of the bus, and everyone stood up to exit. "After you get out, form a single line in front of the red tree."

As I got off the bus, a pebble floated in front of my face. Not in a fast, duck-right-now way, but ever so gently, as if it was a petal floating in calm water. I cupped my hands around it, and immediately the pebble bounced up and down, as if begging to be set free. I opened my palms up to the sky, and it paused for a moment in front of me before floating away.

Eugene was busy running his fingers over the leaves of a nearby bush. "This is surreal. It's like they can sense us."

"The line is over here," Joon said.

In the middle of the forest, surrounded by clusters of tall trees with leaves in different shades of green, stood a lone red tree close to the side of Manisan Mountain. Unlike the other trees in the forest, this one was small and skinny. Maybe a couple of feet taller than Ms. Shin, and she was about average height.

Once we were all gathered in front of the red tree, Ms. Shin took a small pouch from her bag and carefully untied it. Then she sprinkled whatever was inside on the ground surrounding the tree. Instead of floating up like the dirt and pebbles around us, it sank deep into the ground, and the roots of the tree began to grow. One bulged out of the ground right in front of me, and I stepped out of the way. In a matter of minutes, the roots reached the side of the mountain.

The ground rumbled and shook beneath us. I clung tightly on to Joon's arm.

"Stop pulling me down, just hold normally," he said.

I loosened my grip and watched in awe as roots formed a little arch on the rocky side of the mountain.

Ms. Shin walked in front of the arch and said, "Go inside single file, please. It's really narrow." She patted the rocks and said, "Yeolyeora."

Those must've been the magic words: *open, please.* The rocks groaned and moved out toward us, creating a narrow pathway. Where the rocks should've been was a small tunnel leading inside the mountain. It looked pitch-dark inside.

I followed right behind Rae. Joon, Chloe, and Eugene lined up behind me.

Joon patted my back and said, "Yell if you want us to run."

"So not funny," I whispered.

Rae swiveled around to wave at us and then sauntered into the mountain.

Ms. Shin held up her hand and motioned for me to wait. I wrung my fingers together and squinted to see if I could catch a glimpse of Rae, but she was gone.

"Lia, you're next."

I followed the path and stopped in front of the entrance. It looked really dark in there. How was I supposed to see anything? What if I fell down a hole or something?

"Can I have a flashlight?" I asked.

"Just trust the process, Lia," Ms. Shin said. "We're on a tight schedule, so you need to hurry up."

As if I could trust the process. Didn't she know by now that I was a bad-luck magnet? But I knew trying to reason with her right now would do me no good. And besides, there was also a long line of impatient kids waiting for me to go through.

Even though I couldn't see a single thing in front of me, I forced myself to be brave.

I inched forward into the darkness, until it completely enveloped me.

CHAPTER 6

A warm breeze brushed against my cheeks, and my body relaxed. When my eyes adjusted to the dark, small fireflies lit up an even narrower path between stone walls in front of me. I squeezed my body sideways into the shaft, and the coolness of the rocks calmed me.

As the path narrowed, I panicked. I drew in short breaths, but my heart continued to race. My feet refused to budge and remained glued in place.

Get it together, Lia!

I tried to focus on something happy. Except it was way easier said than done. My mind wandered to the suffocating darkness I'd experienced in the portal.

I desperately hoped that this wasn't the same thing.

"What are you doing?" Joon said from behind me. "Are you okay?"

I couldn't have been happier to hear his voice. "I can't move," I whispered. I was partly embarrassed but mostly scared, with a little bit of disappointment mixed in.

"Just do what you always do," he said in a soothing voice. "Breathe."

Thank goodness he knew what I was talking about, and I didn't have to explain it to him in front of everyone. I inhaled and exhaled and counted to three slowly. But as soon as I tried to take a step, I banged my head against the wall and completely froze in place.

"I can't do this, Joon," I sobbed. "You know I hate small spaces."

"Lia, listen to my voice," he said. "What's the worst that can happen?"

Wasn't that obvious? "I'll get stuck here and never make it out alive!" I said.

"Now," Joon said. "Where is Rae? Do you see her?"

"I don't know," I whispered. "It's too dark to see anything."

"Then try to see if you can hear her." He paused and

then continued, "She's not here because she got past this part."

That was true. Rae was long gone.

"So it's not true that you'll be trapped, right?" Joon said.

If she'd gotten out of here, I could too. I breathed in deeply. Warmth returned to my arms and legs, and my muscles loosened up.

I squeezed Joon's hand, and he squeezed back.

I turned my head away from Joon and inched forward, moving one foot at a time. After what felt like eternity, I felt the edge of the rock and exited into a cave-like space.

A few feet away from me stood a spiral staircase that led straight up. So high that I couldn't see the top. There was a small beam of light shining down from above. I stepped onto the first stair, and immediately it started to move.

Oh my goodness. I was on an enormous spiral escalator. Very thankful that I wouldn't need to climb a million stairs to get to the mountain peak.

Joon hopped on after me. "I wish they had this everywhere."

"That would be so fun and convenient," I said. "No cars, no traffic. Just fast-moving magic escalators everywhere."

I held on to the railing and studied my surroundings. The inside of the mountain glistened with stalactites hanging down, just like we'd see in caves. But the ones here resembled sheer crystals. Below us were stalagmites shooting up from the ground—except instead of looking like the typical rock formations, they were made of colorful gems.

Just stacks of stunningly cut blue, green, white, yellow, purple, red, and orange stones. When the light hit the stalactites a certain way, it bounced off and created rainbows.

I stretched my arm out to touch one.

"Hold the railing Lia," Joon said from behind me.

I turned around to face him and said in a pretend serious tone, "Yes sir."

"I'm glad you're feeling better enough to joke around," Joon said with a grin. "But can you face forward, please?"

I stepped down toward him. "Like this?"

He rolled his eyes. "Come on, I don't want my gallant rescue to go to waste."

I turned back around. "I wouldn't describe it as gallant."

"Then what?" Joon asked.

"A good effort."

We both laughed. This was what I missed most about Joon. All our fun and silly moments.

After a few minutes, I passed though the opening at the top of the mountain and stepped off the escalator when it ended. We were so high up that all I saw were the leafy green tops of trees. In front of me was Chamseongdan, a large teardrop-shaped structure built entirely of large rocks stacked one on top of the other.

Everyone who had gone in before me waited near a wooden fence off to the right side of this structure. But I decided to wait off to the side of the escalator.

Joon popped out first, then Eugene and finally Chloe.

"Yeoksi," Eugene said. "Uiri isseo."

That's right. That's me, Loyalty Lia.

I grinned and waved two fingers in front of me.

"Thanks for waiting to explore together," Chloe said.

"Okay, uiri people," Joon said. "Can we go check out this place now?"

I put my arm around Joon's shoulder. "Let's go."

We found everyone mulling around by the fence. When I got there, I realized why the fence was there. Because there was nothing below us, just a massive drop to the base of the mountain.

Joon and Eugene peered over the fence.

"How far a drop do you think that is?" Joon asked.

Eugene shrugged. "You could probably still heal yourself."

Chloe smooshed her face against my arm. "So scared of heights."

"Just look the other way," I said, and gently turned her shoulders toward the structure.

Ms. Shin pointed her finger at each of us as she counted out loud. "Great. All forty-eight of you made it." She glanced at her watch and smiled. "Perfect timing."

That was the first smile we'd seen from her all day. I guess she must've been pretty stressed about getting all of us First Years here in one piece.

"After we go through there"—she pointed to a small gate located a few feet ahead—"I want everyone to stand quietly along the outer perimeter."

We all said, "Ne, Seonsaengnim!"

She nodded in approval and motioned for us to follow her. When she got to the gate, she took her school badge from around her neck and swiped it across the side of the gate. For a really ancient-looking gate, it must've been outfitted with some of our magic technology. Very impressive.

The gate creaked open, and right in front of us was a

large platform smack in the center of this teardrop-shaped area. Across from the rounded wall we all stood against was a pretty steep stone staircase that led to a rectangular pedestal. It looked like an altar or a stage.

Once everyone was inside, we heard the beating of a drum. I searched around for where the sound could be coming from.

From behind the single large tree next to the altar came a man dressed in a black hanbok with white bands around the sleeves and neck, paired with billowy white pants. He had a yellow sash tied diagonally across his chest and a red sash around his waist. When he turned around, I could see that the yellow and red sashes mixed with a blue one that had been used to tie them together, forming a rainbow on his back. He had a janggu, a traditional Korean hourglass-shaped drum, strapped across his shoulder. When he beat both ends of the drum with sticks, yellow sparks flew into the air.

Another man dressed in the same outfit held a brass jing—a large gong—and a wooden stick with a round ball at the tip. As he played the jing, red sparks floated into the air. Two more people danced onto the stage. One had a buk—barrel drum—strapped across his chest, and another held a kkwaenggwari, a small gong. Blue and white sparks fluttered off their instruments as they played.

They came down the steps and filled the area in front of us, dancing while playing the instruments. This must have been a samulnori, a percussion quartet. I'd never seen one in real life, only videos—performed by no-magics, of course. There was just something about the music that touched me to my core. I could feel the rhythm in my bones, as if it had always been a part of me.

It was a joyous and happy sound.

Right when we had gotten used to the dancing, another group of men appeared, dressed in rainbow-colored hanbok and sangmo, traditional Korean hats with ribbons. The musicians continued to play as they strutted backward to make room for the dancers with the hats. As they moved and flipped around, the long white ribbons on their hats created shapes and letters in the air.

Everyone cheered and the music grew faster.

The ribbons seemed to be alive, and the dancers tapped on their hats and shouted, "Wiro." The ribbons detached from the hats and flew up into the sky.

But the music didn't stop. Each dancer knelt down on one knee and raised their hands palms-up toward the sky. I stared up at the sky and couldn't see anything. But the ribbons came floating down toward the dancers, except they were no longer white. They were gold.

The gold ribbons landed gently on the dancers' outstretched hands.

"Why are they gold?" Joon whispered.

"Probably because gold symbolizes the gods," I answered.

There were the four guardian animals in charge of each of the four directions. But there was also a central direction, which symbolized the gods, and the color was yellow. So I bet this was what the gold meant.

The dancers took the gold ribbons, walked up the stairs, and placed them gently on the altar. After they went back down, women dressed in white holding white feathery fans appeared from within the tree. As they sauntered, their skirts rustled and changed to brilliant shades of pink, blue, green, and orange.

At the altar they waved their fans over the ribbons, which slowly melded into one long ribbon. Then the women danced to a different song being played by the musicians. The ribbon floated toward where we were and encircled each person, one by one. When the ribbon wrapped around me and brushed against my face, it was so cool and soft to the touch, like Umma's silk pillowcases, which I'd snuck into my suitcase.

Finally the ribbon floated up and eventually disappeared into the sky. A large rainbow appeared from within the clouds and touched the center of the stage.

Everyone stayed silent for a couple of seconds before the air filled with the thunderous sound of applause and cheering.

Ms. Shin bowed to a group of four people in different-colored hanbok standing at the bottom of the stairs. She shook hands with everyone the polite way, with her left arm supporting the right hand.

One man was wearing a cream-and-green-colored hanbok. His eyes bulged out when he said something to her while jabbing at the sky and whipping his arms back down with such force that Ms. Shin drew back. Then a woman in a white-and-gray hanbok whispered into her ear.

When she walked back to us, her facial expression seemed a little off. But I couldn't figure out what it meant. I wished one of us had the ability to read minds or expressions.

She spoke in such a quiet voice, I strained to hear her over all the chatter around us. "First Years, please go back to the bus and have dinner at Geum San Su restaurant at the bus terminal."

Wait. Was she not coming?

Everyone walked out toward the gate, and I turned to look back at her before I left.

But I couldn't spot her in the crowd anymore.

CHAPTER 7

The trek back down the escalator and through the narrow tunnel went much easier now that I knew what to expect. Also Joon chatted with me the entire way to help take my mind off my claustrophobia. I think in his own way he was being protective so that other kids wouldn't find out about my fear.

Even the ride to the Ganghwado bus terminal felt like a fun amusement park ride when we bounced up and down in our seats. The bus pulled into the parking lot of the terminal. All the seat belts unclicked, and everyone got up as fast as they could, trying to be the first one off.

My stomach grumbled. I couldn't wait to eat, and nudged Joon to get up and move.

"The kids in front of us haven't gone yet."

"I know," I said, "but if you get up, we could squeeze by."

He grudgingly stood up and scooted out into the aisle. Thankfully, the line started to move.

When we got off, Eugene and Chloe were waiting for us at the entrance to the terminal.

"Do you remember what floor the restaurant is on?" asked Chloe.

Of course I remembered. This was one of the other big events I'd really been looking forward to today.

A group of kids crowded around the nearest elevator.

"Follow me," I whispered as I walked to the elevator farther inside the terminal.

The night before, I had scoped out the layout of the terminal.

There were many ways to get to the restaurant. The stairs would've been my first choice, but they were on the other side of the building. Then there were elevators. The elevator that everyone was standing in front of only went to even floors. But this elevator was one of the few that went to odd floors. It was the fastest way to the third floor.

I pressed the elevator button, and it opened right away.

Joon, Eugene, and I walked in.

"I'll meet you there," Chloe said.

I held the elevator door open for her. "Where are you going?"

She looked down and mumbled, "Bathroom."

I pressed the close button a few times and hoped I hadn't embarrassed her.

"Push three?" asked Joon.

"Do you see any other options?" said Eugene.

There were only two buttons on there, and we were on the first floor.

Joon laughed it off and pressed three.

As soon as the door opened again, I shot out. I'd found the menu online and had pored over all the reviews of this Korean-style Chinese matjib. It consistently ranked within the top three on the different food vlogs I followed. It was one of those places where they closed as soon as they sold out of food. According to rumors, they were never open past lunch.

But today was probably a special case, since they were expecting us.

Still wasn't worth risking it.

About a third of the tables were already full with kids from our school. The ajeossi working the counter greeted us and escorted us to a table.

Joon picked up the menu and looked it over. "What's good here, Lia?"

"I think I should order different dishes for us so we can taste everything."

Eugene looked at me with a frown. "Don't I get a say?"

My face turned red. "Of course you do," I said. "What did you want?"

He pointed at the picture on the wall. "Haemul jjamppong."

Joon put the menu down. "I'll let the foodie order for me."

I loved how a lot of Korean restaurants had call buttons attached to each table.

Eugene pressed the button on the table, and soon a server came over with a tablet.

"Jumun hasigesseoyo?"

"Haemul jjamppong, samseon jjajangmyeon, tangsuyuk, geurigo bokkeumbap, please."

Oops. I quickly corrected myself. "Juseyo."

Right as I finished ordering, the door chimed, and a large group of First Years flooded in. I was pretty glad we were part of the first wave of diners.

The server tapped on his iPad and before leaving said, "Muleun self-service."

He pointed to a small table near the back of the restaurant that had a water dispenser with cups.

"Ne," I said.

Joon and Eugene stood up to bring us some water.

Ever since I'd moved to Korea, I'd tried my best to speak Korean to locals here, because not everyone spoke English, so it was the polite thing to do. Also, the ability to blend in was an important part of being a top-tier agent. It was good practice to start early as an agent in training.

Eugene placed a cup in front of me and drank from the other one. Joon set two cups on the table.

Eugene leaned across the table and said, "Did you see Ms. Shin's face?"

I was glad he'd noticed it too. "It was totally strange. What do you think they were talking about?"

Eugene shrugged and said, "My bet is on IMA top secret stuff."

I laughed and shook my head. "That's not even betworthy. So vague."

Chloe slid into her seat. "What about IMA?"

"We're trying to figure out if there's some top secret thing going on," I said.

"Oh, I love mysteries," she said. "I'm in."

Eugene whispered, "Do you think you can hack into the IMA database?"

Chloe almost snorted out her drink. "Can I hack? Is that even a question?"

"That would get us all kicked out," Joon said. "Don't even think about it."

When had he become such a stickler for the rules? This was a post-IMS development.

Chloe ignored him and took out the standard IMA-issue tablet that all of us had. It was twice as big as her phone and just as thick. When she opened it up, it unfolded two times and transformed into a keyboard as the keys popped out ever so slightly. She pressed her finger on the upper right corner of the keyboard, and it powered up. Then she tapped twice on the space bar, and her keyboard got a little thicker and grew a lid, transforming the tablet into a laptop. She flipped the lid up and started typing.

Normally the screen floated in the air and was almost transparent. But when we were in public, the tablets were programmed to look like normal people's laptops so we could avoid unwanted attention.

A few moments later she said with a grin, "I'm in."

"Whoa," I said. "That must be record speed."

She shrugged. "Machines just like me."

"Lower your voices," Joon hissed.

"Yes, sir," Eugene said with a laugh.

Joon rolled his eyes. "If you guys get caught, leave my name out of it."

We all ignored him and huddled together over Chloe's screen.

"Can you search for anything?" I asked. "Like, using keywords?"

She nodded. "Name it. I can find it."

Eugene smiled mischievously. "How about top secret files?"

Joon scooted over next to me to get a look at the screen too. "It's too late for me to pretend I didn't know anything about your hacking."

Chloe furrowed her forehead and said, "Well, looks like I found the files, but I can't get into them."

On the screen was a list of files with a little icon of a bomb next to each. Halix, New Fire, Doctor X, Mission LK, Peach Run, and the list went on in no particular order. There were so many files.

"I thought you could talk to all machines," I said.

She pointed to the small letters next to the icon of the bomb. "These are protected by magic and only accessible by the person with those specific initials."

Eugene's eyes were glued to the screen, and he kept swiping down to read the names of more files.

"What's the point?" I said. "Chloe can't hack into them."

Eugene pulled out his phone. "I'll take notes. Who knows? Maybe something will stand out to us," he said.

"It's all just code names," Joon said. "They mean absolutely nothing to us."

That was true. A rescue mission could be called Apple Tree for all we knew.

"I don't see anything about Chamseongdan or Dangun or Gaecheonjeol in here," I said.

"First," Joon said, "it wouldn't be that obvious. And how sure are we that Ms. Shin's conversation had anything to do with where we were?"

Of course I didn't have any hard facts. That was why we were doing this deep-dive detective work right now. But I couldn't get the facial expression of the man talking to Ms. Shin at Chamseongdan out of my head. When he was pointing at the sky, it was a look of anger.

"Just a hunch," I said.

"And that's an excellent quality for agents in training to have," Eugene said as he high-fived me.

The server returned to our table, pushing a cart of food. Chloe quickly stuffed her tablet into her backpack. Once at our table, the server carefully placed all four dishes in the middle and gave us a pair of scissors, tongs, a stack of four bowls, plates, and silverware.

Joon pulled out napkins from a little wooden box on the table and placed one in front of everyone. Then he passed out chopsticks and spoons.

The jjamppong was a spicy noodle soup with steamed seafood. There was a ring of squid, some shrimp, and then an abalone at the center. I took the tongs and cut the seafood into smaller pieces so it would be easier for everyone to eat. Then there was the jjajangmyeon, which was another feast for the eyes. This one was the typical black bean sauce over noodles, except for the mound of thinly sliced and fried sweet potatoes on top. Joon started to mix the noodles.

In front of Chloe was the tangsuyuk, sweet-and-sour breaded pork on a bed of shredded cabbage. On top of the pork was shredded white radish, which was unique to Ganghwado, then sliced red cabbage on top. Chloe carefully grabbed some of the vegetables on top and moved them over to the side of the plate so she could better mix it all together.

Then in front of Eugene was a bowl of black bean sauce and a plate of fried rice with an egg sunny-side up on top. "Does anyone not want the egg mixed in?" he asked.

"I love the gooey egg," said Chloe.

"Same," we all echoed.

We took turns serving ourselves and gulped everything down.

After we were done eating, the server placed on the table little cups of omija tea, a traditional Korean drink that tasted bitter and sweet at the same time.

Rae walked over and put her arm around my shoulder. "Roomie," she said. "Wasn't the performance so magical today?"

"I loved it too," I said with my biggest smile.

The kids at her table got up to leave. "I'll see you at the bus, then," she said, and hurried over to join them.

"Why were you smiling like that?" Joon asked.

He knew me so well. After all, we'd been friends for almost ten years.

"What was wrong with her smile?" Eugene asked.

"It's her 'I don't like you, but I will be nice' fake smile," Joon explained.

I laughed because that was totally what I would've done in the past. But he was wrong in saying I didn't like her. I'd never shared a room with anyone before, since I was an only child, and I was just more careful around her because I needed us to get along.

"I was just being friendly," I said. "Things with Rae are fine. We're just so different, but that's okay."

The rest of the First Years started clearing out, so we grabbed our backpacks and left.

"I'm going to look for some snacks," Eugene said.

"Find us something yummy," I said.

When Chloe, Joon, and I got onto the bus, Victor waved Joon over. "I saved you a seat."

Joon looked at me and then back at Victor. I didn't want him to sit with Victor, not because I was a jealous friend but because Victor really seemed to have it out for me. What if Joon started to take his side someday?

I slid into my spot and waited for Joon to join me. But

instead he bent down and said, "Would you be really mad if I sat with Victor on the ride back?"

That stung, but I tried not to show it.

"No, go ahead," I said. "Eugene should be here soon with some treats."

"Do you want me to wait with you?"

"It's fine," I said.

Chloe sat down next to me. "I'll sit with her. Don't worry."

"Okay." Joon walked to the back of the bus and sat down next to Victor.

The bus driver asked, "Is everyone here?"

"No," I called out. "Ms. Shin and Eugene aren't back yet."

Eugene hopped onto the bus, carrying paper bags of goodies. He handed one to me and Chloe. "I got us some hotteok."

"Thanks," I said as I took the bag from him.

Eugene stuffed a piece of paper into his pocket.

I took a bite of my hotteok, a popular Korean street food that was a fried pancake filled with nuts, brown sugar, and cinnamon. Instead of being gooey in the center, the inside was grainy and hard.

Chloe must've noticed too because she nudged me and made a face.

"How come these are so cold?" I asked.

Eugene shrugged. "That's strange. The ajumma said she just made them."

I laughed. "You've been duped."

Cold or not, it was still tasty. I took another big bite.

"Have you seen Ms. Shin?" I asked Eugene.

"I thought I saw her by the elevator," he answered.

Thank goodness she was okay. I'd been getting worried about her.

"I thought you and Joon were inseparable," Eugene said as he sat down in front of us.

I turned red and answered quickly, "He's free to hang out with whoever he wants."

"Whatever," Eugene said. "Team Air Check is way cooler. He's missing out."

We munched on our food, and about five minutes later, Ms. Shin walked onto the bus.

The headmaster seemed different, but I couldn't pinpoint it.

"Kids, what a day," she belted in an unusually loud and chipper voice. "Let's go home."

I nudged Eugene and cupped my hand over his ear. "Doesn't she seem a little strange to you?"

He shrugged his shoulders and yawned. "She could just be tired."

I couldn't tell for sure. Maybe he was right.

CHAPTER 8

The next morning I woke up to my alarm without even snoozing it. After washing up, I tiptoed back to the room to finish getting changed. I looked across the room to make sure I hadn't woken Rae up.

I grabbed my backpack and headed for the door.

Rae rubbed her eyes and pulled the blanket over her face. "What time is it?"

"Five a.m.," I whispered. "Go back to sleep."

Hwarangdo practice started at six a.m. every weekday, but I'd been waking up much earlier so I could go to the magic practice rooms to work on my power.

Once outside of my room, I knelt down and tapped my badge against my mailbox. It clicked open. Inside was a bottle of Joon's latest health drink for me and some letters.

No time to check them now. I stuffed everything into my backpack.

I walked past the elevators, which only went to the dorm rooms, and stopped in front of the door at the end of the hall, which had a large seal of a blue dragon.

Above the doorknob were several buttons with the names of different locations within the house. Each house had its own dining hall, dorm rooms, library, magic practice rooms, and battle room. I pressed the square button with an image of chopsticks and a spoon.

As soon as it read my fingerprint, it beeped, and the chopsticks opened and closed while the spoon swooped side to side. There was a clinking sound like gears turning. This door wasn't a portal, though. Instead, with the right combinations, it opened into different areas located inside our house. I wasn't sure exactly how it worked, but it didn't seem like the separate rooms moved. The clicking sound was probably the dorm floor moving to different areas. Also, because this was all magic plus tech, I'd never actually felt the hallway moving. Not even a tiny sway. Pretty amazing.

After a few moments, the door opened, revealing the dining hall. The usual early risers sat at their favorite spots. There was Peter, a Fifth Year, who always sat in the middle of the cafeteria at a small table, eating cereal while flipping through a book that was projected in front of him. A few tables away was Binwoo, who was a Second Year, eating a bagel. She literally created and sat inside a bubble, always deep in her thoughts. Finally there were the twins, Daisy and Rosie, who were First Years like me. They always ate Korean food in the morning and bounced math equations back and forth between each other. They waved and then went back to their work.

I grabbed a banana and walked to my usual table near the window. Within a minute I'd gobbled down my food and speed-walked to the door. I pressed the image of a potion bottle for the magic practice rooms. Once it read my fingerprint, pink liquid bubbled up in the bottle.

The door opened into a hallway, with rooms on each side. Above each metal door was a light, showing whether the room was occupied. A green light meant *available*, and a red light meant *busy*. This early in the morning, though, I always got my first choice, since there was hardly anyone here. I raced to the door with a number eight on it, and sure enough, it was available.

I pressed my badge against a small panel on the wall. It scanned my badge, and then the words *Lia Park, Access Granted* appeared on the panel. I rushed inside and placed my bag on a small table in the corner of the room. The rest of the space was empty so that kids could safely practice their different magic powers. I hadn't measured, but the ceilings were really high for the kids who needed to fly or had other aerial powers.

I opened the newest bottle from Joon and took a sip.

Yikes. This was the worst one ever.

There was only one way to drink this. I pinched my nostrils with my fingers and gulped it down.

Since Joon was a healer, one of the classes he took was medicinal herbs. I never volunteered to be his guinea pig, but he was determined to help me unleash my power. So every day he sent a new mixture through the mail.

A few letters slipped out of my open bag. I unfolded the first one, and my heart dropped.

It said, *Go back to California.*

My hands trembled as I read the next one. *You don't belong here.*

Tears stung my eyes, but I opened the last one. *Mommy and Daddy can't help you now.*

I bit my lip and crumpled up the letters.

Words were just words, right? I knew that but it still hurt. Who would send such hateful mail like this, all typewritten? No way to know who the letters were from. And of course they'd all been mailed anonymously.

Ever since I'd gotten to school, my power had been off, like it had a mind of its own. Super unreliable.

Joon was the only one I'd told about my power not really working.

Sometimes I couldn't help but wonder if what everyone was saying behind my back was right, that I was a fake and an imposter. Maybe my magic had worked only because the jewel had supercharged it. And after I'd destroyed the jewel, my magic had gone poof too. Maybe it had stayed for a while and then eventually worn off. If that were the case, then that would explain so much. Perhaps the only reason I would be allowed to stay if my magic was truly gone was because of my parents. They had contributed so much to the IMA community and were also legendary agents.

I tried to get out of my head, because the more I stayed in it, the more I'd spiral down into a deep hole. It was hard to climb out of it and truly believe with my whole heart that everything was okay, because the only common denominator in all these happenings was me. Nothing like this was happening to anyone else.

Could I have been really that unlucky all those times? Pretty slim, I bet.

But if I wanted to stay here, which I desperately did, I needed to find a way to make my power work before anyone else found out the truth. My biggest fear was that it was fading from within and there'd be no way to restore it, making me a no-magic forever. I shuddered at the thought.

Time to focus, Lia.

This was why I woke up so early every single day.

I took out Umma's journal and flipped to the page marked with a pink sticky note. This was a spell we were learning in class, but I loved being able to supplement with Umma's handwritten notes. She had a lot of good tips, and I could use all the help I could get.

I placed my sweater on the floor and sat down next to it.

"Sarajigeora," I chanted with my eyes closed. *Please, please, please disappear.*

I opened my eyes, and much to my disappointment, my sweater was still there. It hadn't even budged. Not that this was a moving spell, but if the sweater started to disappear and flickered, I bet it'd move at least a quarter of an inch.

I skimmed Umma's notes, and they said, *Tip: Try to imagine where you want the object to disappear to.* They didn't teach us this part in class, actually. All the teacher told us to do was picture every single particle of the object melting away. Not helpful at all.

This time, I pictured my sweater on top of my bed in my room. Wait. Maybe that was too far. The far corner of the room seemed like a much better choice. I shut my eyes and chanted, "Sarajigeora."

Darn it. Still there. The alarm on my phone went off, which meant it was time to hustle. I had less than ten minutes to get to my Hwarang morning training session.

I walked outside the House of Benevolence to the giant blue dragon statue in front of the hyperloop train station, and paused as it scanned me. A second later the eyes of the dragon glowed blue, and I sprinted down the stairs. The doors of the train opened, and I hopped on right before they closed.

Eugene was already seated, so I joined him.

We never specifically said anything about meeting at a certain time, but it had become our morning ritual to meet on the train, and then we usually ran to Hwarang practice together.

Thank goodness for the hyperloop. It saved me so much time. The train stopped, and Eugene said, "Ready?"

"So ready," I said as I bolted out the still-opening door.

I ran up the stairs and waited impatiently in front of the giant red-vermilion bird that guarded the exit.

As soon as the eyes glowed red, I jogged along the walkway.

"You're going to be exhausted even before class starts," Eugene called out.

"Don't worry about me," I yelled back.

My plan was to get just a little ahead of him. Then I'd slow down and pace myself so I wouldn't be worn out for class.

A little bit down the road was a sprawling one-story building with a sign above the doorway, written in Korean and English, that read *Hwarang Center*.

I slowed down to catch my breath and wiped the sweat from my forehead.

Once we were both inside, we quickly changed into our white uniforms. I checked and made sure no one was in the locker room before I retied my hair and adjusted the bobby pins to cover the white streak. We met in the central training room. Everyone sat in ten neat rows on the mat on their knees. I found an empty spot in the front and knelt down.

Posted on the wall was the Five Codes of the Hwarang that we all lived by.

1. Loyalty
2. Filial Piety
3. Honor
4. Courage
5. Justice

Master Leo stood in front of the class. "Good morning."

"Good morning," we all said in unison.

He picked up a jangbong—a long stick—from the weapons rack and tapped it on the floor.

"We'll be focusing on the spin technique using the jangbong."

We hadn't practiced with that one yet. I was excited to check it out.

"Please grab a jangbong, strap on your protective gear, and come back to the center."

Half the kids rushed to the weapons rack, so I went to put on my gear first. I put on my helmet, chest armor, and leg protectors. Then I grabbed a jangbong. It was a lot lighter and wobblier than I'd expected.

A couple of minutes later everyone gathered in the center of the room.

Then Master Leo motioned for David and Sena to come up.

David, a Fifth Year and basically the Hwarang superstar, was the designated demonstration person. I was a direct descendant of Nammo, while Sena, a Fourth Year, was a direct descendant of Joonjeong and the only other Hwarang girl in our school.

Before there even were Hwarang, there were Wonhwa, female warriors. Nammo and Joonjeong were the original two Wonhwa. After their demise, only men were chosen to be Hwarang.

David and Sena bowed to each other, and everyone stood up and formed a large circle around them.

Master Leo said, "Begin."

Sena raised her jangbong and struck David. She took a step back, lifted her stick horizontally over her head, and blocked David's strike by holding it steady. This was the start of a progression of attacks that sped up with each strike and didn't stop until Sena's back was pressed against the wall.

David moved back to the center of the room and waited for Sena to follow. When Sena was holding her jangbong in front of her in a ready stance, David raised his jangbong to strike her. Sena immediately blocked by swinging down with her jangbong. Then she spun around and hit David's leg.

Master Leo tapped his jangbong on the mat. "Excellent demo as usual, David and Sena."

They bowed and stepped back.

"Now pair up," Master Leo said.

Eugene turned around to face me. "You ready?"

I'd always thought I was very coordinated and athletic until I came to this school. Here I had to try much harder and practice more than I ever had before to keep up. But not Eugene. He was super athletic, and it all came very naturally to him. I'd actually never seen him at the practice rooms in the training center.

I moved the jangbong in front of me. "Let's go."

He smiled and swung his stick down. I blocked it with my stick. Then I immediately bent my knee and spun around. I felt a smack on my shoulder.

"You're dead."

I stood up and rubbed my shoulder. Even with the chest armor, it really hurt a lot. "You're supposed to just let me finish."

"But you're so slow," he said with a smirk. "You'd never make it out alive."

He was so annoying. Even if I was slow, Master Leo wanted us all to practice the moves. Keyword: *practice*. Which meant that he wanted us to complete the sequence.

"Let's see you do it."

"Happy to show you how it's done," Eugene said.

I raised the jangbong up in the air and struck down, hitting his jangbong. He blocked my strike and lifted my jangbong up with his. Then, before I knew it, he had spun around and smacked me on the outer thigh.

"Ouch!" I yelled. I caught my breath and massaged where he'd hit me.

Eugene panted and was bent down with his hands on his legs. "You okay?" He was barely able to get those words out, which could mean only one thing.

"I knew it!" I shouted.

"What?" Eugene lay down on the mat and groaned. "I need a minute," he whispered.

I sat down next to him. "You used your power."

He grinned. "But I won, didn't I?"

"You won the battle, not the war." I couldn't believe he would be so selfish as to use his power in a practice session. It totally drained his energy, and he wouldn't be much help as a partner for the rest of the class.

Master Leo came up to us. "Eugene, I told you no magic during practice sessions."

Eugene sat up and said glumly, "I'm sorry, Master Leo."

Master Leo sighed and said, "Lia, I need you to take Eugene to the infirmary."

"But I haven't had a chance to get the spin down yet," I said.

"I know, but there is a Hwarang code," he said. "We take care of our own. And if a person is injured, it is their partner's responsibility to get them somewhere safe."

"Ne," I said. I had forgotten about code number three, honor.

I yanked Eugene up.

"Gentle!" Eugene yelped.

Even though I'd agreed to take him, I was annoyed at how he had totally ruined the practice session for me just because he was trying to one-up me. I mean, didn't he get that we were all on the same team? What was the point of beating me in this one tiny practice lesson?

CHAPTER 9

By the time we got to the infirmary, I was sure my shoulder was going to fall off. Eugene was purposely putting all his weight on me. I was sure he could've walked a little, but he wasn't even trying. I practically dragged him all the way there.

Dr. Janet wore a white coat over a fitted beige shirt with dark green pants. Her hair was swept up in a messy bun when she came out to greet us. "Master Leo said to expect you."

"Eugene used magic and has no energy now," I grumbled.

She put on black glasses with a cat-eye frame and took

a silver pen from her coat pocket. She held it in front of his face. Gold beams shot out and encircled his head, then moved down to his arms, body, and legs. A pretty lifelike 3D image of Eugene appeared before us.

Dr. Janet pointed to something running up and down the 3D Eugene's body. "See this red line here?"

"What is that?" I asked.

"That is our gi," she said. "Energy running through our body."

This was so cool. I knew we all had gi, but it was a completely different thing to see it running through an actual person.

"Well, it's not supposed to be red," she said with a frown. "An easy way to remember it is: red means 'recharge,' green means 'go.'"

For the first time since I'd known him, Eugene looked scared.

He hobbled over to a chair and sat down. "So what's going to happen to me?"

Dr. Janet pulled on a tab on the wall, and a bed came out. "Here, lie on this."

I helped Eugene onto the bed. "Will he get better with some medicine?"

"There's no medicine to cure completely depleted gi,"

she said. "You're very lucky you didn't use it all up."

Wait a second. That wasn't possible if he'd used only five seconds because that was the full range of his power.

"Eugene," I said. "Did you push it today?"

He had a sheepish look on this face. "Maybe a little?"

"How much?"

"Ten seconds," he said quietly.

Oh my gosh. That was five seconds more than his limit. "I can't believe you'd do that!"

Dr. Janet grimaced and said in a stern voice, "There are limits to our power for a reason—because that's all our body can handle."

"But then how can I increase how long I can stop time if I don't take chances and try?"

"I see so many kids like you at the start of the year," she said. "This is why you have power-specific classes. When your body grows stronger, you can handle more. If you're not ready and your body can't handle it, you will die."

I mean, I knew I was an overachiever, but Eugene was way worse. I worried for him. "See, you heard that, right?"

"I will never do that again," Eugene said in a trembling voice. "I swear."

Dr. Janet brought out a large green book from the

bookshelf behind her desk. She scanned the table of contents and flipped to the middle of the book. "Ah, there it is."

She placed her hand on top of the page and rubbed it twice. "Gi hoebok yak."

Never heard of gi recovery medicine before.

I stared at her as she dug her hand into the page and pulled out an IV bag with green liquid from inside the book.

"Roll up his sleeve for me, please," she said.

I did as I was told but watched her from the corner of my eye. She fiddled with the seal on the bag until there was a sound like air being released.

"Suaek nwajuseyo."

The bag rose in the air and floated to where Eugene was lying down. I heard two clicks, and a needle and a tube fell down from the side of the bag. Without warning, the needle jabbed Eugene in the arm, and he winced.

"Don't worry, the pain will wear off soon," Dr. Janet said.

Eugene cringed but listened to Dr. Janet and stayed put.

A lever on the bottom of the bag, which most definitely had not been there before, turned to the right.

Green liquid dribbled out of the bag, through the tube, and into Eugene's arm.

"What is this thing?" he said in a groggy voice.

"It's just nutritional fluid that will recharge your gi faster than if you did it naturally."

"How long would it take naturally?" Eugene asked.

Dr. Janet tilted her head to think. "It depends on how much gi you used. Could be anywhere from a few hours to half a day."

This was so ridiculous. I couldn't believe he'd risked so much of his gi to beat me at one tiny demonstration.

Honestly, I bet he hadn't even known that this would happen, or he wouldn't have pushed his power so much beyond his limit like that. But that didn't make this all better.

"You owe me a practice session."

He laughed. "Deal."

With a gi-fueled-up Eugene, I hustled and made it in time for the first class of the day, Tinkergets. On even-numbered days Tinkergets class was in the morning, and on odd days it was in the afternoon. Today was an even day.

I plopped down next to Joon, and Eugene sat across from me.

"What's wrong?" Joon asked.

Darn it. I should've sat next to Chloe. I hated that he knew everything about me. It was hard to hide anything from him.

I took out my phone and texted him. Just a little annoyed at Eugene but we're good now.

Joon texted back. I told you to watch out for him. He's super competitive.

I thought we all kind of were, in our own ways. After all, our team name wasn't Air Check for nothing.

I replied, Sometimes, I guess. But nothing I can't handle.

Joon shook his head and wrote, I worry about you, Lia.

I smiled and answered, That drink today was the worst. I can still taste it in my mouth.

He laughed out loud and wrote, Sorry. Experimented with a new batch of medicinal herbs.

I replied, I'm practicing every morning, and things are kind of getting better. I knew this was a big fat lie, but I thought it was the best way to get Joon to stop talking to me about it.

He grinned as he wrote, That's great. All your hard work must be paying off.

Mr. Koo, our Tinkergets teacher, stood next to a small table with different objects at the front of the class. "Today each group will select one of these everyday objects and make it do something it's not meant to do."

Everyone started talking at once.

"Quiet, please," he said. "I'll call you up by teams."

He pointed to the first two tables in the front. "Team Exterminators and Team Avalanche."

I still chuckled hearing the different team names. Table one had chosen *Exterminators* because they wanted to gas out the competition. While table two had picked *Avalanche* because they planned to bury all the other teams.

Thank goodness they selected their items quickly. They did have first dibs after all.

"Team Air Check and Team Destroyer," Mr. Koo called out.

Everyone at our table and Victor's got up and speed-walked to the front. On the table there was a comb, toothbrush, toothpaste, paintbrush, ten-thousand-won bill, pen, hand wipes, and socks. They were all so different, but they were all things that were somewhat portable.

"The pen?" Chloe asked.

"Too generic," Joon said. "It'll be hard to be creative."

There were so many cool pen gadgets already out there. Coming up with something new would be challenging.

"How about the hand wipes?" Eugene asked.

"Actually, there's so many things we could do with those," I said.

"Ooh," Chloe said. "Each wipe could be for a different purpose."

Just as I was about to pick up the wipes, Rae, from Team Destroyer, grabbed them. "Sorry," she said. "We liked these too."

"Darn. That was a good one," Joon said in a disappointed voice.

We lowered our voices and huddled around the table so the rest of the class couldn't hear our decision-making process.

Chloe gestured to the toothpaste. "How about this?"

I crossed my arms to form an X. Toothpaste could get pretty messy, and it could leak while we carried the tube around or if we squeezed it too hard.

Joon pointed at the socks. "These could be kind of cool."

Chloe, Eugene, and I each made a big X almost at the same time. Socks were tough, because they wouldn't fit everyone, so there would need to be an additional spell to turn them into a one-size-fits-all item.

"Too hard to program," Chloe said.

"Team Air Check, you have thirty seconds," warned Mr. Koo.

I picked up the paintbrush.

Eugene nodded, and Joon and Chloe made a circle shape with their fingers.

"We selected the paintbrush," Joon said.

"Technically, that is a calligraphy brush," Mr. Koo said.

I guessed that was an important piece of information. Maybe calligraphy brushes were made with animal hair, compared to a regular paintbrush, which had synthetic hair.

We were allowed to start while the other two teams chose their objects.

Chloe and I rolled a cart of supplies with our team name written on it over to our table. Inside each cart were containers of herbs both magical and nonmagical, bottles of chemicals and liquids, potions, microchips, wires, cords, and building tools.

There was a decent mix of normal-people items and

magical items. Because even though we were part of the magical world, we still lived in the normal-people world, so it was important to know how to use everything.

When we sat back down at our table, Eugene and Joon immediately started typing on their keyboards.

"So what should we turn this into?" Chloe asked.

"Let's brainstorm what we could do with the brush," I said.

"I'll type out everything we say," Eugene said.

"That's what I was doing," Joon said.

"I'm faster and a better organizer than you are," Eugene said smugly.

"Fine," Joon said as he closed his keyboard.

"Obviously this was used for calligraphy and paintings," I said.

"Writing, too," Chloe added.

"That's the same thing," Eugene said. "I'm not going to add that."

"Water and ink," Joon said.

This brainstorming session wasn't getting us anywhere. I looked over at Team Avalanche next to us and saw the kids talking excitedly with their hands and grinning. The coder in the group, Joanne, was typing furiously on her computer.

"Come on, we need to be more creative," I said. "What can we make to help agents?"

"We wouldn't know," Eugene said.

"What's that supposed to mean?" I asked.

"He just means, only you two have ever been in the field before," Chloe said.

Joon pointed at all the other kids in the room. "Oh, come on. No one in this class has, and everyone is working together," he said. "Stop making excuses."

"Lia, you know all about everyday nifty objects, don't you?" Chloe asked.

"Yeah," Eugene said. "We heard about how you used all the boring no-magic items to save the day."

I turned red and put my arm around Joon's shoulder. "We did it together."

Joon pulled my arm off him. "But they were your things."

Fine. If they weren't going to be that helpful, I would have to come up with some ideas. Because there was no way I was going to fail this class. I needed to do well. Like, get-straight-A's-this-year kind of well, so that even if my magic wasn't stable, I'd have a good argument for remaining at the school.

I picked up the brush and swiped the bristles over my hand. Then I thought of it.

"Brushes are meant to get wet, right?" I said.

Chloe's eyes lit up. "Keep going."

"What if when it's wet, it can shoot out sparks and stun someone?" I said.

It was a brilliant idea.

"Like a Taser," Joon said. "But how are we going to get it to work?"

Chloe sifted through the basket of microchips and picked out a long, slender one. "I can code it to spark." Then she added, "Obviously not a magic spark, just an electronic response, like when you rub the ends of two open wires together."

"Great!" I said. "I'll look through these chemicals and herbs and figure out how to make it retain moisture."

The easiest method would be to just dip the brush into water. But when agents were out in the field, there'd be no guarantee that they'd be able to find a water source the second they needed it. So even though this way was trickier, I wanted to find the most practical and easiest solution.

"I guess that leaves us to hide and seal the chip inside," Joon said to Eugene.

Chloe waved the chip above her screen until she heard a beep. She handed it over along with a switch to Eugene, saying, "Don't forget to add this, or it won't work properly."

"Good point," Eugene said. "Wouldn't want it to explode on us while we're working."

Chloe laughed. "I'll be coding from my laptop."

Joon grabbed the brush and scooted next to Eugene. They combed through the toolbox to find just the right tool to help them drill a small hole that they could slide the chip into, but it needed to be done carefully or else the wooden brush would completely splinter and break.

I pulled the container of potions and herbs closer to me. The bristles needed to be wet before the sparks happened, but the brush couldn't be wet all the time, because everyone's pockets or bags would get wet, and that would eventually dry the brush out.

Think, Lia!

I grazed my hand over the bottles and read each label carefully, hoping that would help me think of possible combinations. I picked up a bottle of avocado oil, and then it hit me. If I coated the bristles with this, it would store the moisture, but the clothes would get wet and oily.

I spotted a jar of waterproof coating. When I opened it, the substance looked like wax. Bingo! Perfect solution.

"I need the brush for a minute," I said to Joon.

"Wait, we're almost done," he said while holding the brush upside down.

Eugene hovered over him and slid the chip inside the hole they had made at the bottom of the handle. Then he pushed the switch into the slit on the side of the brush.

"They're in," Eugene said.

"Grab the wood filler and put it over the hole," Joon directed.

Eugene grabbed a jar that said *Filler* and used a teaspoon to take out a little of the gray putty.

"Watch out," Joon said. He moved his finger out of the way as Eugene covered the bottom with the filler.

"Now for my favorite part," Eugene said.

Joon picked up a thin electric candle lighter and handed it to him. "Maybe you should take the brush, too."

Eugene chuckled. "What? You don't trust me?"

"Not going to risk it. I know what it feels like to get burned," Joon said. "Hard pass."

"Got it." Eugene put on heat-resistant gloves and held the brush. When Joon clicked on the button in the middle of the lighter, there was a soft hiss of electricity. It sparked a little X-shaped current at the tip of the lighter.

The instant Joon placed the lighter against the putty, it

melted and blended into the wood, creating a transparent cap over the hole.

Eugene carved something onto the brush with a thin pick. He placed the brush down on the table next to me. "It's all yours."

I studied his handiwork and smiled when I saw the letters *LJEC* carved onto the side of the brush.

The switch on the body of the brush was a very small tab. I flicked it on and off with my fingernail.

"Lia, stop playing with that," Chloe said.

"Sorry!" Totally forgot that she was still programming it.

I flexed my hands and got ready to work.

First, I used a pipette to extract some water and placed it in a petri dish. Then I swished the brush around in the liquid, turning it around and flattening it to make sure I got every single bristle.

Next, I rested the brush on the edge of the petri dish. I used a small spatula to take the wax out of the jar. Then I applied it to all sides and covered the tip of the brush. Within seconds the wax hardened to form a soft cover around the wet bristles.

I grinned and slid the brush across the table. "Did it. Team Air Check for the win."

"Done!" Joon shouted as the bell rang.

Mr. Koo beamed and said, "Great work today, class. Those who haven't finished, come by at six a.m. tomorrow to complete your assignment." Most of the kids groaned.

"We'll test these gadgets tomorrow afternoon," he said.

Everyone got up to leave for their next class. "You guys go ahead," I said. "I'm going to run one more test to make sure the water's properly absorbed."

"Are you sure?" Joon asked.

"I'll stay with her and make sure it gets done," said Eugene.

"Thanks," I said. "But go ahead, I'll be fine."

"We owe you one," Chloe said.

How could I have forgotten the most important step, double-checking my work?

I held the brush and touched it against my other palm and felt the smoothness of the wax.

This was it.

I put a little pressure on the bristles, and water dripped down my hand!

It worked.

Thank goodness the switch was off.

I added a little more water and sealed the bristles back up with wax.

Before I left, I wanted to try out one thing. I knew we weren't technically allowed to use our own power, with the exception of coders, but mine didn't really work anyway.

I just wanted to test it out. Maybe a different environment would help. I whispered, "Sarajigeora!"

Vanish, brush, vanish!

Of course, just as I'd expected, absolutely nothing happened.

CHAPTER 10

The rest of the day flew by. It was tough concentrating, because my mind kept drifting to the weapon-selection ceremony tonight. It was the biggest and most important event for First Years.

When it was finally time for the ceremony, I walked onto the field right next to the academic building. The sun had just set, and it would've been hard to see anything if it weren't for the ten lanterns floating in the air.

There was a large stage in front of the bleachers. I passed the crowd of students and spotted Joon in the first row. He'd saved me a seat by putting his bag next to him. The best friend ever. We had always talked about this moment back in California and had different ideas about how weapons would be selected.

I handed Joon his backpack and sat down. "Which one do you want?"

What we wanted always changed. There were pros and cons to each of the three different weapons: bow and arrow, sword, and spear.

"The sword," he said. "But it doesn't matter what I think."

That was true.

What we wanted and what we received could end up being two very different things.

"I decided on the spear," I said.

"I thought you always wanted the bow and arrow."

"Well, the spear is the only one that has two functions. I can throw it and use it as a stick."

"I guess so," Joon said. "I hope there's a way for whoever is handing out the weapons to know what we want."

"Oh! Maybe a psychic will be up there," I said. "And that's how they pick."

"Or it could be totally random."

I doubted that. Something as special as this, something that would determine my forever weapon, couldn't be a simple drawing from a hat.

Ms. Shin walked onto the stage and raised her hand up for everyone to settle down. She didn't speak, but her presence alone made everyone nudge the person next to them, and soon the crowd grew silent.

She smiled brightly. "Good evening. We will be doing our annual weapon-selection ceremony for our First Years tonight." She gestured to the kids sitting in the back behind the last row of First Years. "Thank you for coming out to support them."

Mostly the older kids cheered and whistled. All the First Years clapped nervously, while some sat with their hands clasped together.

Four men dressed in black robes carried a large rectangular wooden box and placed it in the center of the stage. It was very wide and long and was a little higher than Ms. Shin's waist. On the front were four carved hanja characters, with a circular gold border around each one. It was impossible to make out the characters from where I was sitting.

"When I call your name," Ms. Shin said, "please come forward."

I whispered to Joon, "I hope she goes in reverse alphabetical order."

"Doubt it," he said.

Ms. Shin pulled out a silk pouch with red, blue, yellow, gold, white, and black patchwork and loosened the strings. She put her hand inside and threw a bean into the air. Instantly it wrote out the name *Joon Kim* in the air in sparkly green letters. It looked like firecracker sparkles had exploded all over his name.

Oh my gosh. He was the first one.

"Good luck," I whispered, squeezing his hand. I was so nervous for him.

Joon stood up and walked toward the three steps on the right hand side of the stage. He didn't stop until he was standing next to Ms. Shin.

She lifted the gold latch on the top of the box and opened the lid. "Please sit inside."

Joon started to take off his shoes.

"You can keep those on," she said.

I laughed nervously. Poor Joon. Being the first one was always tough. But I was half-relieved it wasn't me and half-jealous that Joon would find out his weapon so soon.

Joon climbed into the wooden box and sat down. The box was high enough that I no longer saw his head once he was sitting.

Ms. Shin closed the lid and flipped the latch down.

Everyone around me gasped.

"Don't worry," she said. "There are holes all over the top of the lid so that it's very easy to breathe in there."

Then she sprinkled what looked like water on top of the box and chanted, "Mugi seontaek jakdong."

As soon as she uttered the phrase, *Activate weapon selection*, the hanja characters that were on the box floated out and formed a diamond shape in the air, with each letter corresponding to the four houses in each corner. Wisdom, benevolence, courage, and strength. Those were the core values that IMA emphasized.

When she'd finished chanting, the water droplets floated into the air and formed a large circle. They spun around and formed different shapes until they turned into a bow and arrow.

The older kids standing in the back cheered, and some raised their bows in the air.

Ms. Shin unlocked the box and nodded for Joon to come out.

"Please stand here with your palms up," she instructed. Joon stretched out his hands, as if he was about to receive a gift.

She spun her finger in the air, and the droplets solidified into a fan and dropped into Joon's hands.

"The bow and arrow have chosen you."

Joon looked confused but held the fan with both his hands.

"Open it," Ms. Shin instructed.

Joon lowered the clasp at the top that held the fan together. As the fan opened, it started to move. Different panels stacked on top of each other and then curved around until they were in the shape of a bow. The second he reached out, it morphed into a real bow, and several arrows clunked onto the ground.

"Be wise, courageous, and strong," Ms. Shin said. "Always search for what is true."

Joon gripped the bow and arrows as he walked off the stage to his seat.

"Yours looks so cool," I said.

He was beaming. "I actually love it."

The bow and arrows were pretty big and took up a lot of space. "How do you turn them back into a fan?" I asked.

He pressed the bow between his knees and tried to push it down with his hands. "I have no idea."

"Try saying something to it," I suggested.

"Close."

Nothing happened.

"Uh. Fan."

Still nothing.

"Nothing's working," he said. "I'm sure Ms. Shin will show us later."

He placed them on his lap and let go. As soon as he was no longer touching the bow and arrows, they whirred in his lap and folded back into a fan with a dark green handle.

"That's so neat!" I shouted.

People around us turned to glare at me, and I mouthed, "Sorry." I had been so excited about Joon's weapon that I hadn't even noticed that the next person had just received her spear.

I clapped and waited for Ms. Shin to pull another name from her silk pouch. *Please call me. Please. Please. Please.* I didn't know how many spears there were, but if it was a limited number, maybe my chances would be better if I was called earlier.

Ms. Shin tossed a new bean into the air, and it sparkled into *Lia Park*.

It was me!

I stood up and ran to the stage. Everyone laughed, but I didn't care. I just couldn't wait to find out what my weapon would be.

Ms. Shin opened the lid and motioned for me to climb inside. "Sit with your legs crossed or straight out. Whichever feels comfortable to you."

Once I'd climbed in, I leaned my back against the side of the box and hugged my legs. The inside was actually pretty roomy and more comfortable than it looked from the outside. It smelled like a forest.

Ms. Shin closed the lid, and I heard the clunk of the clasp being fitted back on. Little red beams shot out from the top and sides of the box. They aimed at my head and slowly enveloped every single part of my body to my shoes. The beams disappeared and a glowing orb appeared. I covered my eyes with my arm because it was so bright.

It said in a deep voice, "Lia Park, Hwarang, daughter of Chung Mira and Park Minwoo."

"Yes," I whispered.

After I answered, it burst into a fiery ball, and the voice hissed, "You will never be safe." It fell and set the floor on fire.

I shrieked and pounded on the lid with my fist. "Open! Please let me out!"

Ms. Shin opened the box and stared at me with confused eyes. "What's wrong, Lia?"

The fire, the voice. It was all terrifying. I got out of the box as fast as I could and pointed inside. "It's on fire!"

She looked inside and said, "There's nothing in here."

What? That couldn't be. I couldn't have imagined the ball trying to set the box on fire. And the creepy voice. I peeked inside the box and put my hands inside. Not only was the box not on fire but the sides were very smooth and cool to the touch.

It was impossible.

Three of the men in robes spread out through the area, waving what looked to be a metal detector, but little drones that looked like bees flew out from it and hovered above the field. The fourth man walked around the box and chanted under his breath.

Everyone in the crowd stared at me and whispered. I could hear what they were saying all too well.

"Her again?"

"She must be cursed."

"Is she seeing things?"

"Remember she passed out at the train station?"

"She should just go home."

I fought to keep a poker face, but tears puddled up in my eyes. My face turned warm. I swiveled around and tilted my head up to keep them from falling. A robed man whispered something into Ms. Shin's ear and then exited the stage.

"I know you are worried, but security has cleared the box and this field," she said. "We will continue with the ceremony."

Ms. Shin lifted the lid of the box and motioned for me to get in. "The selection was incomplete."

I wished she would just give me the spear and be done with it. Would having a different weapon than what I was meant to have really matter? Did she not understand that I had no intention of being inside a box of fire again?

From the crowd I heard Joon shout, "You can do it, Lia!"

A few kids laughed, but I spotted my Hwarang brothers and sister in the back with their weapons in the air. They chanted my name, and soon everyone else followed their lead.

I forced a smile and climbed back into the box. I really had only one choice, because if I refused to get in, the ceremony would be over for me, and I'd be singled out even more.

As I sat inside, huddled in a corner, a more frightening thought crossed my mind, causing me to shiver: What if I really had imagined the voice and the fire? Every single time something went wrong, Ms. Shin checked, and everything turned out to be normal and functional.

Was it really me? Was I the problem?

But that went against everything I had studied over the years, and since I'd been at IMS, I'd learned that an agent's instincts were key. If something felt off, it was off, 99.9 percent of the time. If only I had a way to prove it. I missed Umma and Appa. They'd know exactly what to do and say to make me feel better.

For a moment, I wished I could cast the boho spell over myself, creating a shield around me, but then remembered how unreliable my power was. What if by some miracle it did actually work, and somehow because of that the selection failed? Then I would have to do it all over again, not to mention face the wrath of all the annoyed kids who hadn't gotten a chance yet.

I cringed as the beams encircled my body again. Then, just as before, the orb appeared and spoke my name. I covered my face with my hands and glued my back to the side of the box, making sure I was as far away as possible from where the fire had started last time. Instead of the sparking of flames, I heard cheering.

The lid opened, and I breathed in the fresh air.

A sword made of water droplets spun in the air above me.

Once I'd gotten out of the box, Ms. Shin handed me a folded silver fan. "The sword has chosen you."

The silver handle of the fan felt unexpectedly cool in my hands. I loosened my grip around it and flicked it open.

A thunderous boom filled the air, and the left wing of the academic building burst into flames.

CHAPTER 11

All the lights on the entire campus blacked out, and the lanterns flickered off. I clutched my new sword tightly. All I could hear were kids screaming and teachers shouting at them to sit down. Ms. Shin walked in front of me on the stage, held up her badge, and shouted to the students, "Bisang baljeongi jakdong."

Electrical currents ran up and down her badge, but she didn't flinch. From every direction came a whirring sound. Then the lights in the floating lanterns came back on. I looked around to see where the sound had come from, but everything looked as it had before.

Except the burning building that was still on fire.

Ms. Shin spoke with authority. "Please sit down, everyone."

After a few minutes, all conversations stopped and there was complete silence.

"I activated the emergency generators," Ms. Shin said. "They will keep the lights on in all our buildings until we figure out what is happening."

Someone in the crowd shouted, "Are we under attack?"

Instead of answering the question, she said, "Please remain seated until I come back."

Then she pressed a transportation coin against her badge and disappeared right in front of our eyes.

I gently dropped my sword onto the stage and watched it transform back into a silver fan. At the very top of the fan, the latch clicked shut. I picked up my fan and hurried over to my spot next to Joon.

Like everyone else, Joon was too busy staring at the fire to even notice that I was back.

"Maybe it was an accident," I said. "Or faulty wires."

He turned to look at me. "You're not serious, right?"

Okay. Maybe it was just me hoping for a normal school year. Looking at the school on fire brought back memories of our house getting blown up and everything that followed after that. It was a lot, but we'd managed to survive and had gotten into our dream school. It was a grueling journey here that I didn't want to repeat.

"Impossible," I said, trying to convince myself. "There's a protection barrier around the school, remember?"

He sighed. "Which was obviously broken."

There was no way anyone could get in past the school's protection barrier. It was impossible for students to even sneak off campus. Once you were inside the school, there was no way out except past the security guard and the two haetae sculptures. Though they were sculptures, I was convinced there were cameras or secret recording devices in the eyes, because I never could shake off the feeling of being watched.

"You don't know that," I said.

"Want to bet on it?" said Joon.

I chose not to answer him, because if he was right, what would that mean? I shuddered at the thought.

"Where's Chloe and Eugene?" I stood up to look around at the other kids sitting in the bleachers.

Chloe was sitting a few rows back with some kids from her house. But Eugene was nowhere to be found.

"I saw Eugene by his locker right before I came here," Joon said. "He's probably here somewhere."

That was true. Knowing Eugene, there was no way

he'd skip out on this. I expected him to be sitting in the first row to make sure he didn't miss out on the action.

Joon nudged me and pointed at the other end of our row. "He's right there."

Sure enough, there he was. We were on the other end of the same row. But I could've sworn I hadn't seen him when I was up there on the stage.

There was a loud whooshing sound like ocean waves were crashing down on top of us. A few teachers stood near the burning building with their hands raised up to the sky. Another group waited behind them. Hundreds of buckets dumped water onto the building. Then they sat upright for a minute or two as they waited to be magically refilled. Then they began dumping water again. After a few turns, the teachers switched places with the other group. They looked worn out and sat on the grass as they recharged.

After what felt like an eternity, Ms. Shin finally reappeared on the stage. She raised her identification card in the air and said, "Haetae bokje sijak."

Was she talking about cloning the two haetae sculptures that were out by the front of the school?

From the darkness, one of the haetae sculptures appeared, except it was no longer a statue. It had come to life as a robot, which began to multiply and clone itself. The second haetae sculpture bounded in with the guard from the front gate riding on its back, the guard Appa had referred to as the first line of defense. In a matter of minutes there were at least a few hundred haetae scattered along the edge of the field, and they continued to surround the school. There seemed to be an endless supply of them.

"Boho gineung jakdong," Ms. Shin said.

The horn on the head of each haetae straightened up, and golden rings floated up from the horns into the night sky. They formed so fast and there were so many that I couldn't count them all. When the rings bumped into each other, there was a little flash as they linked. Soon there was a chain of golden rings creating a protective dome over us.

"I enacted our school's breach protocol," Ms. Shin said.

This was bad news, which could only mean something must've gone terribly wrong.

"One of our haetae cloned itself, and they're situated around the perimeter of the school. Their function to protect has been activated." She pointed at the gold chain above us. "This will keep us safe until we can get the barrier working again."

Kids shouted their questions. I had a million things I wanted to ask too.

Ms. Shin blew a whistle, and I cringed at the high-pitched sound. But that did get everyone's attention.

"Let me finish, and then I will take questions," she said.

Two robed men rushed onto the stage and set up a table. They placed a tablet on top and left.

Ms. Shin placed her finger on the tablet, and a large screen appeared in the air. She clicked on the first icon. An image of a rusty circular object with decorative markings showed up on the screen.

"This is one of the three heavenly heirlooms," she said. "The mirror."

Heavenly heirlooms? Was she talking about the ones from the play in history class that had been separated and hidden away forever? Because they were dangerous?

She continued, "The mirror was hidden at our school."

How could anyone think that a school would be a good place to hide a sought-after superpowered treasure?

"But it has been stolen."

"No way," I whispered.

"See, I told you something was wrong," Joon said.

The next image was of a smashed lantern in the transportation room.

"The intruder used this portal and then destroyed it," Ms. Shin said.

So that's how they must've gotten in and out.

"Who do you think stole it?" I said.

"If you stop talking," he snapped, "maybe we'll hear what she's saying."

Jeez. He didn't have to be so mean about it. This was all very shocking news for everyone. I mean, IMS was supposed to be one of the safest places. Things didn't make sense.

A different image popped up on the screen. This time it was of a monster with a lot of heads. I counted four heads, but I bet there were some in the back.

"This is Jihagukdaejeok, also known as the King of Darkness." She pointed at the heads. "It has nine heads."

She flipped to the next slide, which had nine blacked-out photos, with a red border around the ninth picture. "Nine heads means nine identities. The King of Darkness can take the identity of a human being. One identity for each of its heads. The ninth identity is the monster itself."

Oh my goodness. So basically it was like a super-morphing monster with nine lives.

Then she pressed a button, and red *X*s appeared over some of the photos. "The good news is that IMA has eliminated seven of its identities over the years," she said. "But the bad news is that the eighth identity is unknown and still at large."

Ms. Shin continued, "And we have every reason to believe it was the one who stole the heirloom. We must recover the two remaining heavenly heirlooms from where they've been hidden before the King of Darkness steals them, too."

"He looks so scary," I said.

"Surreal," Joon said.

But Ms. Shin wasn't finished. "I know this will be challenging, but we need all hands on deck right now."

For what? I hoped she didn't want us to hunt the King of Darkness down.

"We need two teams to recover the heavenly heirlooms," she said.

Some kids chatted excitedly, while others looked scared and shocked.

"Of course we will provide you with all the support and intel you will need to be successful," she added reassuringly.

"Who gets to go?" shouted Victor.

"We will figure out how to select the teams tomorrow," she answered.

The next slide popped up on the screen. It was a burnt electrical panel with a lot of the wires pulled out. "This box on the wall was what kept our school safe."

An image of a short, broken wooden stick filled the screen. "Someone used this to fry our panel, causing the fire and breaking the barrier around the school. If anyone has information regarding this object, please come find me after."

I squinted and looked closer at the image. There was a faint carving of the letter *C* on the wood. It couldn't be.

Joon gasped and whispered, "Is that . . ."

It sure looked like what was left of our paintbrush from Tinkergets class. But that was impossible. How could it have gotten there? No one really knew what our brush did except for us and the teacher.

Mr. Koo walked up to Ms. Shin and whispered something into her ear. Her expression changed from worry to fear.

"Everyone, please go back to your houses," she said. "Those of you who have not selected your weapons yet, please come to my office tomorrow morning."

Everyone got up to leave, but Ms. Shin and Mr. Koo quickly walked over to where Joon and I were sitting on the bleachers. "Lia, Joon, Chloe, and Eugene, stay behind," Ms. Shin said in a loud voice.

I sank lower in my seat and tried to ignore people staring at me as they left.

Joon hunched over in his seat. "This is so embarrassing."

"But we didn't do it," I said. It might have been our project, but I definitely had not fried the panel with it.

"No one's going to believe us," he said.

Eugene and Chloe came over and sat down next to us.

"Can you believe it?" Chloe said. "It does look like our paintbrush."

"Where were you?" I whispered to Eugene.

"I just got held up finishing some homework," he said. "You know me, the overachiever."

He kind of was, but it did seem strange that he'd be late to something as important as this. That didn't seem like him.

Ms. Shin held the remaining part of the paintbrush with a gloved hand and pulled up a chair in front of us. "I want you to look carefully at this and tell me if you recognize it."

Eugene took the stick from her and ran his fingers over the bottom. His face froze.

I grabbed the stick from him and looked at it. It

couldn't be. There was part of the letter *E* and all of the letter *C* inscribed on the broken end. "How is this possible?"

"So it is yours?" Ms. Shin asked.

Chloe reached over and took it from me. She rolled the stick between her hands. "Yes. I can sense the chip I programmed inside."

"Impossible," Joon said as he stared at it.

"Explain to me exactly what this is supposed to do," Ms. Shin said.

"We selected the calligraphy brush," Joon said.

"The brush part is missing," I added.

"Please answer the question. What does this do?" Ms. Shin asked again. "And who did what?"

"I coded it so that it would create an electrical current," Chloe said in a soft voice.

"Eugene and I put the chip inside," Joon said. He pointed at the broken end of the brush. "As you can see, we did a good job, because it's still in there."

Ms. Shin turned to look at me. "And you?"

"I made the brush hold the water," I said. "It helped activate the brush's stun function."

"And did any of you use your own magic?" she asked.

Everyone shook their heads.

"Not really," I whispered. "I just wanted to see if my spellmaking power would work."

Ms. Shin frowned. "Lia, you know we aren't allowed to put our own magic into these gadgets, because First Years' powers are all underdeveloped and too unstable to put into these projects."

"I didn't. The magic wasn't related to the project . . ." I hesitated, unsure if I should continue.

Joon shook his head and grimaced.

"Because my magic hasn't been working well," I whispered. "So I knew it probably wouldn't work, but I just wanted to check."

"Did it work?" Ms. Shin asked.

"No," I said. "It didn't."

"Now, who was the last one to touch the brush?" she asked.

"It was me," I said. I had stayed behind to double-check that the wax I applied worked. I was the last one to touch it.

"But I left it in the classroom," I said. "Someone else must've taken it after I left."

"Let's go with that theory, then," Ms. Shin said. "But who else knew about what this brush could do?"

"Only us," Chloe said. "And Mr. Koo."

This was not looking good for me at all. Everyone

was mad at me or disappointed. Which was honestly way worse than just being angry with me.

"I swear I didn't do it," I insisted. "I left the brush on the table and went to my next class."

"I know," Ms. Shin said. "It had to be a combination of things, including powerful magic, to bring down our protective barrier around the school. And like you said, your power isn't working well now."

It stung to hear her say that, because her words made it real. I was glad she believed me, but it was purely because I didn't have the skills to pull something like that off.

CHAPTER 12

The next morning I wore my black training pants, a fitted shirt, and a light jacket, and tied my hair up in a ponytail. Today was the mission selection, and I really hoped that I would get picked. Of course, it would've been better if the school had never gotten attacked by the nine-headed monster's eighth head. Gross. I got chills picturing a monster head bouncing up the stairs.

But until we recovered the heavenly heirlooms, everyone was in danger. I wasn't sure what the King of Darkness wanted to do with the heavenly heirlooms, but if they had been hidden away, it was probably because of monsters like him. And if he was after the heirlooms, that would no doubt be very bad news for all humans, those of us with magic *and* no-magics. School would never be the same. But if I helped bring one of the heirlooms back, it would be the perfect chance to prove that I belonged here. So I had to be chosen for one of the teams today.

By the time I got to the field, there were maybe fifty students there, less than 20 percent of the school had showed up today. First Years were eligible to compete, but most decided not to join. All missions had big risks, and I guess to a lot of the students it wasn't worth the risk. Less competition for me.

I spotted Eugene and Chloe and hurried over to join them.

There was a line of chairs on the side of the field. Ms. Shin sat in the middle, and there were two men sitting on each side of her. I didn't recognize them, but I could tell by their suits and the way they held themselves that they must have been from IMA headquarters. On the other side of the field stood an impossibly large blanket that defied gravity and was maybe two stories high and almost as wide as the field. I bet it was related to what we had to do today.

Ms. Shin stood up and said, "Hope you all slept well, because you'll need to be in tip-top form."

Everyone clapped and cheered. This was what we had been training for.

"There will be a single challenge, which you will do as a team of four. Each team must have one member from each house, because only then will you be able to use the powers of Obangsaek to recover the heirlooms."

I'd heard about Obangsaek but had never seen it in action. Obangsaek was an ancient Korean five-color theory where the colors white, black, blue, red, and yellow were associated with the five directions (east, west, north, south, and center). Combining the colors of the four main directions would make a team especially powerful.

"When you find your team, join hands and stand in a circle," Ms. Shin said.

Lucky for us, all four of us were from different houses. Eugene was from the House of Strength, Chloe from the House of Wisdom, and Joon from the House of Courage.

Without a word, Eugene and Chloe each grabbed one of my hands. I almost cried, because I knew it meant that even though they heard my secret yesterday, they still trusted me and chose me to be on their team.

"I know you two the best," Eugene mumbled.

"We love you too, Eugene," Chloe joked back.

"Where's Joon?" I asked. He had been standing right next to me just a minute ago. "Let me go look for him."

I weaved through groups holding hands and spotted Joon. I couldn't believe he was holding hands with Victor and David.

I tapped his shoulder and tried to use my calmest voice ever. "Joon, what are you doing?"

He shrugged. "They really needed a fourth person."

"Basically, no one wants to be in a group with you, Lia," sneered Victor.

David, the fifth-year Hwarang, said, "It looks bad for you, Lia. And as Hwarang, we are supposed to protect."

When was I ever not protecting? "But I haven't broken the Hwarang Codes," I said.

"Not true," Victor said. "Code one, loyalty to IMA, and a duty to protect our world."

"Which I'm still keeping," I retorted.

Sena, the fourth-year Hwarang who was also part of this group, said, "Everyone is saying you sabotaged the electrical panel and let the monster in." She paused, then added, "I worked so hard to earn the respect of our brothers. I won't let you ruin that."

"Unnie! I would never do that," I said. All these accusations were just getting ridiculous now. I really respected Sena and thought of her as a big sister. It hurt the most that people I cared about actually believed these lies. I was furious that Sena felt that she needed to prove her worth to be considered equals with the Hwarang brothers. "How about you two keep code three, honor, and trust the goodness of your Hwarang sister?" I snapped.

Joon said sheepishly, "They just wanted to know who was the last person seen with the brush."

"First of all," I said, "I didn't sabotage the electrical panel. You should know better than that."

"The truth has a funny way of always coming out," Victor said.

"And this group is already doomed," I said angrily. "You can't even follow basic directions."

Was this really my friend Joon? I couldn't believe he'd sell me out like that. It was one thing to want to be in their group, but a totally different level of betrayal to tell them about the brush. How could he throw me under the bus like that?

"You know what?" I said furiously to Joon. "You belong here."

I stormed back to Eugene and Chloe. "Joon found another group."

"What?" Eugene shouted. "Baeshinja."

"A total, complete traitor," I said.

"Why would he just leave us like that?" Chloe said as she rubbed my back. "I know you two were close. I'm sorry."

"Isn't it obvious?" Eugene said. "No offense, Lia, but he wants to be on a winning team."

"It's fine," I said.

I had no time to feel sorry for myself. We needed to find a fourth member from the House of Courage, or we'd be disqualified.

Ms. Shin walked around, checking how things were going. She poured oil onto the head of every member of the group next to us. Then she said, "Obangsaek ui him."

The power of Obangsaek. I couldn't wait to see what it was.

Red, blue, white, and black light shot out from their hands and intertwined with a gold that sprang out from the center of the circle.

The light faded away and Ms. Shin smiled approvingly. "We've got our first team to compete for a chance to go on the mission."

She walked up to our group. "Where's your fourth member?"

"We're still looking," I said.

"Which house are you missing?"

"House of Courage," Eugene answered.

She turned to face the crowd and shouted, "Anyone from the House of Courage want to join this group?"

Some people looked around, while others pretended to be very busy fixing their shoes or straightening their shirts.

"Well, I'm sorry," she said. "Your group needs a fourth member to participate."

Joon trudged over hesitantly and grabbed my hand and Eugene's. "I'm with them."

I had so many emotions boiling inside me, but talking to Joon would have to wait. Chloe and Eugene glared at Joon. If looks could kill, as they say.

"Okay, that works." Ms. Shin sprinkled oil onto my head. It didn't drip down onto my face; instead, it sort of melted into my head. I felt a tingling sensation on my face, and then it coursed through my body.

"Obangsaek ui him," she shouted.

My hands started to tingle like there was something under my skin. A blue light shot up from them. All of our colors were so distinct and beautiful. The gold mixed with the red, blue, white, and black, creating a sort of braided bracelet. It circled around us and clasped together, forming a complete circle. Then it faded away.

"We have our second team!" She motioned for us to join team one by the chairs.

Eugene was the first to talk. "Why'd you come back?"

"It's because that team had two people from the House of Courage," I said. "He had nowhere else to go."

"Is that true?" Chloe asked.

Joon glared at me. "Yes, but I wasn't sure which group to choose."

"Why?" I was so mad, I spat out the word.

"Because you're all my friends," Joon said.

"Such a lame answer," I said.

"Am I not allowed to have friends other than you?" Joon said.

"That's not what she's trying to say," Chloe said as she stood in between Joon and me.

"If you're such a loyal friend, you wouldn't be friends with people like Victor," Eugene said.

"What, just because you don't like someone, I'm banned from being their friend?" Joon said. "That's nonsense."

This conversation wasn't going anywhere, because he refused to see what Victor was really like.

"Fine," Chloe said. "We forgive him, right?"

"Maybe if we get to go on a mission," Eugene muttered.

"Lia?" Chloe gave me a look telling me to hurry up and answer.

Didn't Joon see how Victor was trying to break our friendship? I hated to admit it, but Victor was strategic and skilled at spellmaking. There was no way he hadn't realized that Joon was in the same house as him. I bet he had asked Joon to be on his team on purpose to hurt me. And I was even more upset at Joon for falling for it.

I knew Eugene was furious for me because to him, loyalty and honesty were everything. Chloe didn't really have any other friends except for us. It was so like her to want to just move on and have everyone get along again. Our peacemaker.

We were already bound together by the Obangsaek. So what if I was still mad at Joon? I couldn't let Chloe and Eugene down. They'd stuck by me when Joon had bailed, and I knew how much they wanted to go on this mission.

"Sure," I said. "Let's do this."

Half a smile crept onto Joon's face. "I won't let you down."

Eugene rolled his eyes. "Whatever."

After Ms. Shin had bound all ten teams with the power of Obangsaek, she spoke into a floating microphone, which just followed her wherever she went. It would disappear when she wasn't talking and reappear when she was ready to start another speech.

"The two highest-scoring teams will be assigned missions," Ms. Shin said.

She walked toward the blanket. "Boyeojugeora."

The blanket dissolved, revealing ten stations. Each station had a large vase on the ground and a table. Every single vase had nine smaller vessels of different sizes attached to different spots on the large vase. Placed on each table was a piece of paper and ten arrows, with different-colored feathers tied to the ends. In front of the table was a yellow line painted on the field.

"This is the IMS version of the game tuho."

Tuho was a traditional Korean game played by the royals and yangbans, the ruling-class families. The objective of the game was to get as many arrows as possible into the vessels. There was no doubt in my mind that the rules of this challenge were going to be very different.

"You will work as a team and try to get arrows into the vessels," Ms. Shin explained. "Scoring will depend on the size of the vessel and the type of arrow used."

She snapped her fingers, and a large screen with all the game details appeared. "Magic is allowed on each other or the objects. But remember the IMS student handbook rule: Killing is forbidden. Do not harm to kill."

Kill each other? Was she joking? Why would we do that when all we needed to do was toss some arrows in?

"Rule number two: All arrows must be thrown from behind the line, and the vessel cannot be moved." Ms. Shin paused and added, "Invisibility and time-stopping powers are also not allowed."

Eugene groaned and was joined by a few others.

"All teams, please go find a station," Ms. Shin instructed.

There were ten teams and ten stations. Everyone rushed to get a good spot. The vases all looked the same to me. I was just about to follow Joon and Eugene when Chloe pulled me aside.

Chloe passed me a small pink box with a red bow. "Here."

"What is it?" I asked.

"Just hurry and open it."

I pulled the lid off the box. Inside was a gold necklace with a star pendant.

"It's so pretty," I said, hugging her.

She pointed to the same exact one around her neck. "It's a friendship necklace."

I took the necklace out of the box and put it on. "Thank you so much, Chloe."

Joon and Eugene were shouting and waving their hands for us to hurry up and come over.

Once everyone was settled, Ms. Shin held up her badge and drew a number ten on it. "You have ten minutes to strategize, examine, and figure out how to maximize your powers."

The scoreboard at the left of the field powered up. It beeped and started to count down.

I grabbed the arrows and passed them out to everyone. "See if you notice anything on them."

The arrowheads were smooth, sharp, and typical, but at the ends the feathers were all different. I laid the three arrows I had down on the grass, sorting by feather.

"Here," Joon said, handing me his. "I have two striped ones and one dotted."

I placed them down next to mine.

Chloe said, "These two have paint splatters on them."

After setting all ten on the grass, we saw that there were three arrows with polka dots, five with stripes, and two with paint splatters.

Eugene brought over the piece of paper that was on the table. We huddled around him and read the scoring sheet, which looked really complicated.

Point System:

Vessels

2 Extra-Small: 5 points

3 Small: 3 points

4 Medium: 2 points

1 Large: 1 point

Arrows

5 Striped: x1

3 Dotted: x2

2 Splattered: x3

"I don't get it," Eugene said.

I picked up a paint-splattered arrow and placed it in one of the two extra-small vessels. "So basically, this would be the highest score combo we could get."

"Which is?" Eugene said.

"Five points for the extra-small vessel multiplied by three, since it's the splattered arrow," I said.

"Giving us fifteen points," Chloe added.

Joon threw the splattered arrow. Instead of moving in a straight line, it zigzagged, soared up, dipped down, and spiraled down onto the grass. No wonder that arrow was a times-three multiplier.

"Try the dotted one," Eugene said.

I picked it up and tossed it, hoping to make it in. The arrow spiraled the entire way until it fell against the vase's side. This was not going to be easy at all.

"Last one," I said. When I aimed the striped arrow at the large vessel, it soared through the air the way a normal arrow should and satisfyingly clunked inside.

I jumped into the air and raised my hand up to give everyone a high five. No one gave me a high five except Joon.

"You know that's the lowest score possible," Joon said. "One point for the large vessel multiplied by one for the striped arrow."

"Equals a whole whopping one point," Eugene said.

Chloe, who had been silent this whole time, rummaged through her bag and pulled out black chips the size of a fingernail. "These are like magnets that I can program." She held a pile in each hand. "If we can somehow attach the positive magnet to the arrows and the negative side to the vessels, then no matter how we throw it, it'll have to go in."

Joon gave Chloe a hug. "You're a genius." He took the ones in her right hand and ran to the vessels.

Eugene took the others and sat down on the grass next to me. I took a chip and wrapped the feather around it. But it was impossible to get it to stick by tying it on. The feather was too short.

"Chloe," Joon said as he placed a chip on a vessel and let go. It tumbled to the ground. "Can't you program them to stick?"

"If I could," she said in an annoyed voice, "then I wouldn't need to be on a team, now, would I?"

For a moment I had forgotten that I still had my pouch of knickknacks with me. Even though I had gotten into the magic school, I'd refused to get rid of it. And it was a good thing.

"I can superglue them," I said.

"Who carries around superglue?" Eugene said.

"Of course you do," Joon said with a laugh. "Lia's backpack is like convenience store meets stationery store. She carries around a ton of random stuff."

I was getting slightly annoyed that he was making fun of me. "I didn't hear you complaining the last time I used it to save us."

"Ohhh," Eugene joked. "She got you good."

"Can we focus, please?" Chloe snapped.

The timer in front of us buzzed with a one-minute warning.

I dug out the superglue from my bag and popped

the cap open. "I'll put the glue on everything."

Joon raced over next to me. "Eugene and I will attach everything."

Chloe smiled and rubbed her hands together. "And I'll program them."

I knelt down on the grass and squeezed the glue onto each arrow, making sure that I covered enough area for the chip to fit. As soon as I was done with one, Eugene and Joon took turns securing the chip on. Chloe whipped out her tablet and began programming. I'd never seen her type so fast.

The buzzer for the timer went off, and everyone put their hands up as a sign that they were done.

I hoped we had finished in time.

CHAPTER 13

Ms. Shin spoke into her floating microphone. "Ready or not, we will begin." She walked around to each team and stuck a sticker on their table. When she got to a team of older kids, she inspected the vase and frowned. "Disqualified for moving vase closer." It was so obvious that they had, because the grass was indented where the vase had originally been placed. The kids shrugged, and she motioned for them to leave the area and join the ungrouped kids watching on the sidelines.

"Can't believe they would make a mistake like that," Eugene said.

"Strange that they did," I said. "They knew better."

Chloe squinted. "Isn't that the group you were going to be with, Joon?"

Joon turned red and said, "Yeah, I guess Rae took my place."

We were the last station to be checked. Ms. Shin examined the arrows and vase and gave us a sticker. I could've sworn I saw her smile a little. Maybe that meant we were on the right track.

"All right, remember the rules," Ms. Shin instructed. "Everything else is fair game. Except, of course, don't kill each other."

Of course we would never hurt—much less kill—each other. Before I had time to think much about what she'd said, a shrill bell rang.

"You have twelve minutes," she said. "May the best team win."

I grabbed a splattered arrow and drew my arm back.

"Wait," Chloe shouted, and held my arm. "You have to tell me which vessel you're aiming at so I can command the chips."

That totally made sense. Whew. I'd almost cost our team a big one. "Extra small, right side."

Chloe squeezed her eyes shut and put her fingers on the sides of her head. "Done."

"Here goes," I said. The arrow soared into the air, zigzagged all over the place, and then swooped down straight into the extra-small vessel on the right.

"Yes!" Joon shouted. We all jumped around and hugged each other.

Eugene grabbed the other splattered arrow and said, "Extra small, left side."

Chloe nodded and said, "Go."

I clenched my fists and watched his arrow swoop up into the air, deep-dive down, and spiral its way into the second extra-small vessel.

We gave Eugene high fives. This was going to be an easy win. I looked around and saw a few groups struggling and others pointing in our direction.

"Eight minutes left," Ms. Shin said.

"Okay," I shouted. "Let's hustle, team."

We took turns with the arrows and shot them all successfully into the vessels. With three minutes left we were down to two striped arrows, and the extra-small and small vessels were completely full.

There was a shattering sound, and the vessels at

the station near us started to burst one by one.

A girl shouted, "Stop it!" to Victor, who was chanting with his eyes laser-focused on the vase.

He smirked and shrugged. "Oops!"

"Tell him to stop!" the girl pleaded to Ms. Shin.

Ms. Shin shook her head. "It's allowed."

Victor's eyes met mine, and I looked away quickly. He was on the team right next to us, so we had to finish before Victor had a chance to destroy our vessels.

Joon grabbed one of the striped arrows. "Medium, top right."

As he was about to throw it, the bottom right medium vessel shattered. "Lia, do your protection spell," Joon yelled.

Uh . . . What was he talking about? He knew my magic was broken.

Victor smirked and continued to stare at our vase and chanted.

Chloe shouted, "Do it now!"

I yelled, "Boho," and a protective half dome appeared over just our vase, leaving an open space for us to still shoot our arrows.

Joon shot the arrow into the medium vessel right above the one that had broken.

I stared in shock that my power had worked and the spell was holding up fine. I was so relieved and happy that it seemed to be back.

I grabbed the last arrow and said, "Medium, bottom left."

Chloe gave me a thumbs-up. The dome wobbled and flickered, which meant it was doing its job as a shield against outside attacks.

All of a sudden, I felt like something was squeezing my neck. I couldn't breathe! I fell to the ground, trying to grab at whatever had me in a hold.

Joon rushed next to me and yelled, "Foul!"

Ms. Shin said to Victor, who was staring me down, "No killing."

"Of course, Ms. Shin," he said, and walked away.

I gasped for breath as the force around my neck was released. But then the grip tightened again.

Chloe shouted, "Victor is still doing it!"

Victor stopped and yelled back, "I'm not killing her."

Ms. Shin narrowed her eyes at Victor. "Two-second rule. Longer than that will be seen as hurting to kill."

Chloe squatted next to me. "Do you need help getting up?"

"I'm fine," I said with a cough. "Keep going."

Eugene grabbed my arrow to throw it.

"That's against the rules," shouted David from Victor's team.

"He's right," Ms. Shin said. "The person who first grabbed the arrow has to throw it."

I took the arrow from Eugene. Just as I was about to throw it, I felt the grip tightening around my neck again. I lifted the arrow as high as I could and said *Idong* in my head. I imagined the arrow swooshing into the vessel. It left my hands and clinked inside just as the buzzer rang. I begged for my power to keep working.

Joon and Chloe helped me up.

"Are you okay?" Joon asked.

I gasped for air and looked for the scoreboard. "Did we win?"

Joon hugged me and said, "Oh my gosh. I'm glad you're okay."

There was the caring friend I knew. Being at school here had changed him. But this was the Joon I'd missed. And I really hoped that he had seen what kind of person Victor was.

Ms. Shin huddled with the judges as they tallied the scores.

"Those jerks," Eugene muttered. "Victor was playing so dirty."

"Yeah, he totally was," Chloe chimed in.

"I guess we're about to find out who the winners are," I said.

Ms. Shin stood in the center of the field. "We tested for the ability to think and act quickly, strength, and teamwork." She smiled and then said, "We're proud to announce our two teams."

A beam of light shined down on the team that had been attacking everyone with magic. "Team one will be Victor, Rae, David, and Sena."

No one cheered for them.

Then the spotlight beamed down on us.

"Team two will be Lia, Joon, Eugene, and Chloe."

No one cheered for us, either.

"Please go back to your houses," Ms. Shin said to the crowd. "And the two winning teams, join me in the library."

"We did it!" I shouted. "Group hug!"

We put our arms around each other, forming a circle, and danced around.

"Team Air Check for the win!" I shouted.

"Can't believe the other team won too," Eugene grumbled.

"Who cares," Chloe said. "We made it."

◆ ◆ ◆

The library was located on the other end of the building from where the fire had happened. Even so, it was strange that the fire hadn't really spread to other parts of the building. It had just charred the entire wing where the power panel was located.

When our team got to the library, Ms. Shin and the other team were already standing by the checkout desk.

"All in good fun," said Victor as he held up his hand to me.

He had some nerve, acting like he hadn't almost killed me. But I refused to show my anger, and I slapped his hand hard. "No worries."

"Before we go on," Ms. Shin said, stretching out her hand to us, "give me your badges."

I stared at her, puzzled, because on the first day of school we'd been told that our badges should be like a second skin to us. Most importantly, we were never supposed to take them off.

The other kids took their badges off and handed them to Ms. Shin. It must have been okay if the headmaster was the one asking, so I lifted the lanyard off my neck.

"Now we can begin," she said. "Follow me."

We walked past all the bookshelves to the back of the library, where the rare books and relics were said to be stored, except it just looked like a few desks with lamps. There was no sign of anything remotely looking like books. It was a temperature-controlled room surrounded by fireproof and magic-proof glass. Because there was no door, it was hard to really call it a room, more like a very large display case.

Ms. Shin pressed her badge and then her palm against the glass. A door appeared, and she opened it for us. "Don't touch anything inside."

The inside looked really different from what we'd seen on the other side of the glass. There were actually tables and pedestals holding relics, scrolls, and books.

The headmaster walked to the first table on the right and placed her hand under the table. The floor planks in the aisle between the tables disappeared, revealing a staircase.

We followed her down the stairs and were greeted by large screens mounted on the walls, control panels, and desks. In fact, it looked like a larger, fancier version of our Park family headquarters back in California.

"This is our school's IMA headquarters," she said.

There was a large wooden table in the middle of the

room with chairs all around it. "Have a seat and let's begin," she said.

We each pulled out a chair and sat down.

"Victor, Rae, David, and Sena," Ms. Shin said as she handed a folder to each of them. "Your mission is to find the second heavenly heirloom and bring it to IMS."

She swiped their badges against her tablet and handed them back.

A three-dimensional image of a dagger spun in the middle of the table. The dagger looked like a violin with a bumpy ridge running down the center.

Then Ms. Shin turned to me and gave me a stack of folders to pass down. "Lia, Joon, Eugene, and Chloe, your assignment is to locate and bring back the third heavenly heirloom."

Ms. Shin did the same thing to our badges and then gave them to us.

The dagger faded away, and a rattle appeared in its place. The rattle looked like an eight-pointed star. But bells were attached to the eight points. A sunshine made from a pattern of straight lines was etched onto the center of the rattle.

Inside our folders was a detailed document about the rattle, names of contacts, and a list of safe houses.

"What happens if we fail?" I asked.

"We can assume the nine-headed monster, Jihaguk-daejeok, aka the King of Darkness, is already in possession of the first heirloom." She paused and said, "It is imperative that you retrieve both remaining heirlooms and return with them to IMS."

"But will they be safe here?" David asked.

"Could we take them to headquarters instead?" I asked. "After all, the King of Darkness was able to steal a heavenly heirloom from here."

"No," Ms. Shin said. "We have increased our security, and it will be impossible for intruders to get in now."

"And if we fail?" I pressed. "Why does he want them?"

"I'm not sure you have the clearance to know," she said.

"With all due respect," Sena said, "we are putting our lives on the line, if by some chance we run into him."

Thank goodness both teams were on the same page about this.

"We deserve to know what's at stake," I said.

Ms. Shin paused and then spoke very slowly, as if she didn't want us to miss a single word. "He wants to plunge our world into darkness and release all the monsters we have caught but could not kill," she said. "And if you fail, our world will cease to exist."

WHAT? What about Umma and Appa? There was no way I would let anything happen to my family. Never again.

Unkillable monsters roaming around sounded horrible. These were the super evil ones that wreaked havoc wherever they went.

Countless agents had sacrificed their lives to catch and seal these monsters away in the Pit. The Pit was hidden in secrecy, and only the top IMA people knew of the exact location.

Failure was not an option in this mission at all.

Ms. Shin must've seen the look of horror on my face, because she quickly added, "Don't worry, you most likely won't run into him, because the adults are on missions to locate the King of Darkness. Our student teams will just be focused on retrieval of the heirlooms."

Somehow, she didn't seem that convincing.

"In the packets, you will find the last known location of each heirloom. But be warned, you will face trials once you get there, before you can find where exactly the heirlooms are hidden."

Now it made sense why we'd had to do the tuho challenge. And of course the heavenly heirlooms wouldn't be somewhere anyone could just go and dig for them. This was a very high-stakes treasure hunt.

"Because you are officially assigned to this mission," she said, "you have clearance for a few more things."

She passed out earpieces, translucent Ping-Pong balls, and small walkie-talkies. "These are for communication with each other. There should be an app on your phones named Project HH. When you open it, you will see instructions on how to check in."

"What if we forget?" Chloe asked.

"There are four of you," she said. "Designate one person now to check in."

Victor and I raised our hands and volunteered.

"Perfect," she said. "Don't forget to create and enter your team name."

"Are we checking in with IMA?" I asked. I wondered if this was like a status report that real agents did.

"You will check in with IMA, but more important, between the two teams," she said.

"But wouldn't that be a waste of time, since we're on different missions?" Rae asked.

"No," Ms. Shin said. "It's all one big mission, and what you see can help the other team."

I picked up a Ping-Pong ball. "And what are these?"

Ms. Shin placed a ball in her hand and gently tossed it into the air. Instead of falling back down it floated and glowed.

"These are your IMA version of flashlights," she said.

Such a nifty idea and so very pretty.

Joon held up his walkie-talkie. "Aren't these kind of old-school?"

"Those are the best backups, because they're not wired or dependent on general magic or batteries to work." She motioned for Joon to test it out.

He pressed a button on the side and said, "Anyone there?"

His voice echoed on Eugene's, Chloe's, and my walkie-talkies, just like a regular one would.

"I don't see how this is special," I said.

Ms. Shin chuckled. "These are bound by Obangsaek and will work as long as you're all alive."

"So distance won't matter?" Eugene asked.

"Correct," Ms. Shin said. "Unlike your typical walkie-talkies, these will work regardless of how far apart you are."

How cool! I was starting to really enjoy being bound together by Obangsaek.

Ms. Shin passed out rectangular leather pouches to all the First Years. "We didn't get a chance to hand this out, but it's a weapon holster."

This made so much sense because as soon as I'd let go of my sword, it had turned back into a fan. If I was ever in a battle, those few seconds of reopening my sword could mean the difference between life and death.

"How do we do this?" Chloe asked. "Our weapons are all different sizes and shapes."

"Just put your fan inside," she instructed. "Then later when you take it out, the pouch will transform on its own to fit your weapon."

"So we just need to pick up the dagger and bring it back?" Sena asked.

"Yes," Ms. Shin said. "All the other information you need is in your folders."

"This is going to be a breeze," Victor bragged. "Want to bet we come back first?"

Had they not been listening to a single word Ms. Shin had said? This was going to be much more complicated than a simple pickup and drop-off.

I rolled my eyes at him. "Just come back alive, okay?"

Victor chuckled. "I think the other team's scared."

"David," Ms. Shin said. "Get your team in order."

David nudged and glared at Victor. "Ne!"

"Go grab some food, pack what you need, and meet in the transportation room in two hours," Ms. Shin said. "And don't forget your weapons."

CHAPTER 14

I felt nervous being back in the transportation room because obviously the first trip had been a disaster. Whatever the reason was, I just hoped that it had been taken care of. But it didn't make me feel any better that we weren't told in advance where we were actually going.

IMA had a deal with the Korean government. In exchange for restoring and protecting cultural artifacts and historical sites, IMA would have unlimited access to them—as long as we didn't raise suspicions among the no-magics and didn't harm or break anything beyond repair. Since most of the historical sites were located in areas of school field trips, IMA sent us on missions near those locations, since no one would think twice about kids roaming around.

When I arrived, Ms. Shin looked down at her tablet and then directed me. "Go to the fourth row, fifth lantern on your right."

"Ne!" I walked down slowly and made sure to count so I wouldn't get lost. Couldn't risk going to the wrong place all by myself.

By the time I got to the fourth row, I spotted Joon and Chloe waiting in front of the lantern.

"Do you have any clue where this will take us?" Chloe asked nervously.

"No idea," Joon said.

"Must be top secret," I added. "It is a heavenly heirloom, after all."

Eugene finally arrived with the largest backpack I'd ever seen. I knew I was an over-packer, but he was way worse.

"Did you fit your entire room in there?" Chloe joked.

"Trust me," Joon added, "it's better to pack light."

Eugene shrugged. "Don't come running to me when you need stuff."

I put my arm around his shoulder. "Don't worry. I get it."

The other team was nowhere in sight. Maybe they had already left or were waiting at the other end of the room. Not only was the transportation room massive but the lanterns were very bulky, so it was hard to see beyond our immediate row. I couldn't even spot the lantern the intruder had smashed.

I texted Umma while I waited. I got picked to go on a mission.

She wrote back right away. I heard from Ms. Shin. Be very safe. Watch your surroundings. In and out, really fast, okay?

Don't worry. Gotta go, I replied.

Ms. Shin's heels clicked on the floor, and we all stood up straight and quieted down.

She looked at her watch and said, "Perfect timing."

"Where are we going?" I asked.

"You will be going to the Seokguram Grotto in Gyeongju," she answered. "It is now five p.m., so it should be closed to the general public. And make sure you ring the bell."

She looked down and checked our shoes. "Good. You are all wearing sneakers."

I held in my laughter. Of course we were. For missions, sneakers were a must. No open-toed shoes, heels, or dress shoes. In fact, some very smart agents in training (like me) packed an extra pair of sneakers in their bag in case the first pair got wet.

"Do you all have your weapons?" she asked.

I unzipped my jacket to reveal the leather pouch, which held my fan. It doubled as the perfect cross-body bag.

"Check!" I said.

Eugene, Chloe, and Joon also showed off their new weapon holsters.

"Excellent," she said. "I hope you never have to use your weapons. But better to be prepared."

Then Ms. Shin tapped on the side of the lantern and drew four straight lines with her finger. The number four appeared in green. "All of you can go in at once. Just sit down in each corner and you'll be fine."

I walked in and sat at the far right corner.

The maximum capacity must have been four or five. Maybe one more person could sit on the pouf in the middle. There really wasn't much room for more people to squeeze in.

Once we were all seated, Ms. Shin peeked inside. "Don't forget, you are stronger together."

"Ne!" We all gave her a thumbs-up.

She waved and closed the door.

"Is everyone ready?" Joon asked as he stood up to press the button.

I clutched my bag in front of me. Even if the lantern glitched, at least we were all together. "Go for it."

Joon pressed the button, which immediately turned yellow. The lights inside the lantern turned off. Unlike last time, there was absolutely no rocking or jerking. The lanterns ran off energy and magic, so the ride was actually supposed to be pretty quiet and smooth. Something had definitely gone wrong last time.

Less than a minute later, the lights turned back on.

"We made it," I said.

When Chloe opened the door, red and orange leaves fell on top of her head. A few branches reached in through the door.

We were in the middle of a forest. Once we had left the portal, I saw that the glass lantern reflected what was around us so well that unless we ran into it, we wouldn't even know that there was something here.

A few feet ahead there was a small incline that led to a dirt road up above.

I took a hiking stick from my bag and unfolded it. "This way," I shouted.

Eugene laughed and tapped my stick with his. "Great minds."

"Over-packers for the win," I joked.

Once we got to the dirt road, I recognized where we were from the pictures in my textbook. We had just passed the ticket booth. If we followed this path, it would lead us to the Seokguram Grotto, which was designated as National Treasure Number 24.

Up ahead was a large pavilion with red pillars and a roof that curved up at the tips. Inside hung an enormous bell and a wooden log.

Oh my gosh. Was that the bell Ms. Shin had told us to ring? For some reason this whole time I'd pictured a doorbell.

Joon stood in front of the bell. It was about three times as tall as him.

"I guess this is it," said Eugene.

"I don't see anything else," Chloe said.

Joon and Chloe stood on one side of the log while Eugene and I positioned ourselves on the opposite side.

"One, two, three," I said.

We swung the log back and forth. It was a lot heavier than it looked. The log hit the bell, and a low gong filled the air.

I scanned the area, but no one was around.

"Ms. Shin didn't say wait," Joon said.

Good point. If she'd needed us to wait, she would've instructed us to.

"Let's just go, then," I said.

We continued walking down the path, which narrowed.

On either side of us were large trees, which were now all changing into their fall colors. The path was on a bit of an incline, but I dug my stick into the ground and pushed myself forward.

Chloe panted, "I almost want to use my spear as a stick."

"You should," Joon said. "No one's here."

"I don't want to ruin it," she said. "And besides, it's too heavy."

Eugene and I hiked side by side, while Joon and Chloe trailed behind us.

"What do you think is up there?" Eugene asked.

"I know there's a lot of sculptures," I said. "But no one's allowed inside anymore."

My mother had told me that back in the day, when she was a kid, they used to let tourists inside and they were able to touch the stone sculptures. These days, from what

I'd read, the grotto was completely sealed off by a glass wall to protect the sculptures inside from moisture, condensation, and visitors.

"But you know IMA has different access," Eugene said.

I hoped he was right, because I really wanted to see the sculptures up close and walk through the grotto like Umma had.

We followed the trail in silence until we reached a gray stone staircase with wooden railings. The staircase was winding, but above us there was a traditional Korean structure that provided the outer shell for the Seokguram.

My legs burned as I climbed up the uneven steps. They were bumpy because they were made of gray rocks. I turned around and said, "Watch your step so you don't twist your ankle."

Because I was in the lead, it was my responsibility to let everyone know what the situation was and what was up ahead.

The landing was so close. Maybe twenty more steps. "We're almost there, I think."

I pumped my arms and marched up the steps until I reached the top. A traditional Korean structure with a winged roof and the dark red wood typical of Korean architecture covered the entrance to the Seokguram Grotto.

I sat down on a bench in front of the structure and drank some water while I waited for the others to join me.

Joon placed his backpack next to me and flipped through his phone. "So according to the documents Ms. Shin gave us, this is the entrance."

I would have been surprised if any one of us had actually brought the paper documents with us on a mission. It was common sense and also IMA rules to store all information you needed regarding a mission in a secure folder on your phone.

Chloe stood in front of the entrance and pulled on the chained door. "Well, it's closed and no one's inside."

At the bottom corner of a signpost near the entrance, which explained the history behind Seokguram, was an outline of a small rectangle. It appeared to be about the same size as our badges. This must have been what Ms. Shin had meant when she'd said she added access points to our badges.

"I think this is it," I said. Once everyone huddled around me, I removed my badge from my wallet and placed it inside the outlined rectangle.

Without warning, the entire structure, gate, and signpost disappeared. All that remained was one step that led inside. Even from here I could see the giant seated Buddha sculpture all the way in the back.

"This is so cool," Joon said.

"Can you believe we get to see these treasures up close like this?" I walked toward the entrance to the grotto.

Chloe followed behind me. "But where do you think the heirloom is hidden?"

"Definitely not out in the open," Eugene said.

Right as I stepped inside the rectangular antechamber of the Seokguram Grotto, I was amazed at the beautiful, intricate, and delicate stone sculptures that were carved into the stone walls all around the entire place.

The first four sculptures were of the Guardian Kings, placed in the front to ward off evil spirits from entering the main chamber. I ran my fingers over the first Guardian King. It was unbelievable how realistic and detailed they looked.

"Don't touch anything," Joon warned.

But it was too late.

CHAPTER 15

Four men dressed in black suits emerged from the Guardian King sculptures.

"State your business," said the man in front of me.

"We're on an IMA assignment to bring back one of the heavenly heirlooms," I said, and showed him my badge.

"Can you tell us where to find it?" Joon asked.

The men chuckled. Another one asked, "Did you think it would be that easy?"

"How do we know we can trust you, anyway?" asked Chloe.

"Fair point," he said. "We are the Guardian Kings."

"So," Eugene said. "Do you even know where it is?"

I nudged Eugene. He didn't have to sound so aggressive.

"We are the protectors, and only those who pass our trial are worthy of knowing the location of the heirloom," said one of the men.

So basically, we had to prove our worth. "We will pass, if you give us a chance," I said.

Joon grabbed my hand and whispered, "Stop agreeing to things. We don't even know what we have to do yet."

"What if we fail?" Chloe asked. "Which we won't," she added.

The men took off their suit jackets and placed them gently on the ground. "You die, of course," one of them said.

Die? Ms. Shin had said this was a recovery mission. She had not mentioned that failure meant . . . death!

"I think there's been a tiny misunderstanding," I said. "We just need to do a trial and bring the heirloom back."

"Yes, of course," said another man. "But the trial may cost you your life."

"We need a minute," I said.

We huddled together and looked each other in the eyes.

"What choice do we have?" I said.

"We can't go back without even trying," Eugene said.

"But trying could mean death," Chloe said as she shivered.

"We will just have to do our best not to die," Joon said.

"I think we were tested and picked for our skills," I said. "So we should be able to pass the trial."

"We'll do it," Joon said.

The men walked past us out of the Seokguram Grotto. They snapped their fingers, and a net appeared. It was higher than a tennis net. With another snap of their fingers, they were dressed in gray sweats and white shirts with the numbers *1, 2, 3,* and *4* on them.

At least it was easier to tell them apart now.

Joon and Eugene gave each other a high five. I guessed they knew how to play this game.

Number One said, "We will play a game of jokgu."

I'd heard of the game but never actually played before. It was first invented around the 1960s and to this day was a popular game. It was kind of like a mix of volleyball and soccer. Each team had four players, and the goal was to get the ball over the net—but you weren't allowed to use your hands.

"Whoever scores three points first wins," said Number Four.

Chloe raised her hand and asked, "What about magic?"

They chuckled. Number Three said, "Where do you think you are? Let's put it this way: if you don't use magic, you probably won't win."

Joon motioned for us to come closer together. "Do you know all the rules?"

"We can use our feet, head, and the rest of our bodies except for our arms and hands," I said.

"And don't forget," Chloe said. "We get three passes to each other before we have to get it over the net."

How did she know that? Pretty impressive.

"Only one bounce between passes," added Eugene.

Number Four threw the ball over the net toward us. I stared in horror and shrieked as the ball soared through the air and then turned into a spinning ball with razor blades attached. As it was about to hit the ground, the blades disappeared and then reappeared.

I ran away from it and linked arms with Chloe.

"What kind of jokgu is this?" Joon yelled. "No wonder they were talking about people dying."

"This is ridiculous," I said in a shaky voice. "There's no way we can beat them."

When the razor blades disappeared, Chloe picked up the ball and closed her eyes. "There's some tech involved, but I won't be able to communicate with it until the blades come out."

"Oh great," Eugene said. "After it slices us up."

"Maybe you can tell the blades to go back in and not come out," I said. "Like ever."

"I doubt it'll be that easy," Joon said.

"You can go first," said Number Three.

Chloe handed the ball to Eugene. "Just use your magic. And don't die."

He nodded and kicked the ball over the net. Number One waited for the blades to disappear and kicked it up into the air to Number Four, who waited for it to bounce and then rose into the air and used his chest to pass it. Number Three used a force from his hands and smashed the ball across the net.

Joon shouted, "Mine!" and bounced the ball off his head. He just missed the razor blades.

Chloe closed her eyes and shouted, "Now," and then I kicked the ball to Eugene, who jump-kicked it over.

Number Four rose into the air and kicked the ball down across the net. I lunged for it but missed.

"One to nothing," shouted Number Three.

Chloe patted my back. "It's okay. We got this."

"Thanks," I said. "No holding back. We have to use all our magic."

"Got it," said Eugene.

Number One kicked the ball over the net. Eugene was about to kick it when Chloe yelled, "Not working!" The razor blades were out, and Eugene stood there just staring at the ball. Joon pushed him out of the way and kicked it with his shoe.

I cried, "Idong," and flung the ball across the net, catching the other team off guard.

"One to one," said Number Four.

"We did it!" I jumped up and down.

Chloe yelled, "Time-out!"

"Three minutes," said Number Four.

Joon sat on the ground, and blood gushed out from his ankle. "Yakson," he said, and the wound slowly disappeared.

"I'm so sorry." Chloe examined her fingers and wiggled them. "My power wouldn't work."

"It's okay," I said while hugging her. "They probably blocked your magic. I think the blades are on a timer."

"Yeah," Joon said. "They also don't come out when you're holding the ball or serving."

"Great job, everyone. Here's the plan," Eugene said. "I'll freeze time for three seconds."

I shook my head. "You were just at the infirmary, Eugene. You can't."

"That's because I pushed myself to my max of ten seconds." He pointed at his watch. "See this? I can set a timer for three seconds."

"Okay. Just be careful you don't overdo it."

We ran into formation, and Chloe kicked the ball over the net.

Number One used his shin to lift the ball into the air. Then Number Four pressed his hands out toward Number Three, who rose into the air and spun the ball using a power force. It swooshed down over the net.

I yelled, "Mine," and ran to kick the ball, but the spinning blades appeared. I froze.

Before I could even react, Joon rushed over and kicked it for me, a second before the ball—and the razor blades—hit my face. Eugene was in midair and then all of a sudden was finishing the spinning Hwarang kick, and the ball smacked down right over the net.

Eugene rushed over to Joon. "Are you okay?"

Joon winced as his wound began to glow orange from

his healing powers. "This one went a little deep, but nothing I can't fix."

"I just blanked out because of the blades." I shook my head. "I'm so sorry."

"I'm fine, Lia," Joon said, getting up. "Let's just win this."

"Great time-stopping trick," Chloe said. "We only saw the start and end of your moves."

Eugene beamed and said, "I added the spin kick too."

"Maybe we can try to time our moves," I said.

"Brilliant," Chloe said. "I'll keep track."

"One to two," said Number Three as he kicked the ball over the net.

Chloe flicked the ball up with her shin and shouted, "Blades." They whirred and disappeared for a split second after the ball hit the ground. Eugene kicked the ball up, and Joon smacked it over.

Number One hit the ball with his head. Number Two's hands turned into fiery balls, and he aimed them at the jokgu ball, which burst into flames as it sailed over the net.

"Fire!" I yelled, holding my arms out to keep my friends from coming near.

The fireball landed on the ground with a hiss, and

when the fire burned out, it looked like the regular jokgu ball again.

Number Four chuckled and said, "Two to two."

"Time!" Joon yelled.

"Three minutes," Number Four said. "Use them wisely."

"How are we going beat a random razor-blade ball that can turn into a fireball?" Chloe moaned.

"I can use my idong spell," I said. I was getting pretty good at it now.

"Great," Eugene said. "Then Joon and I will kick it over."

"We can do this," I said. If we won this game, then we'd be able to find the heavenly heirloom, take it back, and help stop the King of Darkness.

Joon put his arms around my shoulder and Chloe's. "Team huddle and chant."

I put my arm around Eugene. "Go, Air Check!"

Everyone said "Air Check" at a different time. We'd have to work on that.

"To your positions," Chloe ordered.

Eugene whispered something to Joon, and they patted each other on the back.

"Ready?" I asked.

"Whenever you are," said Number One.

I kicked the ball with the top of my foot and shot it across the net.

Number Three lifted the ball in the air using a power force, and then Number Two turned the ball into a fireball again and flung it across at us.

I yelled "Idong," but the ball wouldn't move. "Boho," I yelled, and a shield formed around the ball. I stuck out my foot and kicked it straight up in the air. Eugene yelled, "Now!" and Joon ran toward him. An airborne Joon smashed the ball into the far corner of the opponents' court.

"Score!" Eugene shouted as he helped Joon up. They gave each other a high five.

"Yes!" Chloe shouted, and did a silly dance around the court.

"What happened?" I asked. The last thing I remembered was Joon running full speed.

"It was amazing," Joon said. "One second I'm running, and then the next I'm high up in the air staring at the ball coming straight at me."

Eugene was getting so good at packing in a lot of things within the five seconds of stopped time.

"You're welcome. I tossed you into the air." Eugene waved his hand and bowed. "From the master time stopper."

"We won!" I screamed. It felt so good to shout that out loud. For a moment there I'd been taken off guard because someone had blocked my idong spell.

Number One walked toward us. "You all played a great game, proving you are worthy."

"Thank you," I said.

Number Two snapped his fingers, and the black suits reappeared on their bodies.

I loved my power but wished I also had the ability to change outfits with a snap of my finger. A truly enviable magic.

They walked back inside the Seokguram Grotto.

The last one turned around and smiled. "The answer is not out here. Come in."

We walked past the statues of the Guardian Kings and into the inner chamber, which was round. In the center on a square pedestal was the huge statue of the Buddha we'd seen earlier.

The men stretched out their hands to the arched window near the ceiling and waited. Mist seeped into the room through the window. I coughed and tried to wave it away. It was hard to see anything though this. When the dense fog lifted, the men were gone.

I gasped and pointed at the Buddha. "Look!"

A gem had appeared on his forehead.

CHAPTER 16

E ven though it was now dark outside, the gem sparkled and glistened, lighting up the entire room. All the sculptures that were covered in shadows in the back came to life as the light bounced off them.

I pulled out my phone and scanned the file we were given to see if there was any information on what to do next. "It just says to use our Obangsaek ui him to find the location of the heavenly heirloom."

"One problem," Chloe said. "We don't know how to do that."

"Except we do," said Joon.

I nodded at Joon. "Just like we did at school, we have to all hold hands."

We stood in a circle and chanted, "Obangsaek ui him."

Nothing happened. "We don't have the oil Ms. Shin put on our heads," said Eugene.

But it shouldn't have mattered. Ms. Shin had mentioned that once a group was tied together with Obangsaek ui him, they would be able to channel it as needed.

"Just keep chanting," I said.

I gripped Joon's and Chloe's hands and chanted as earnestly as I could. Our voices filled the room and echoed and echoed. Then an odd thing happened. The echoes grew louder than our actual voices.

It was as if our voices were bouncing off the thirty-nine sculptures on the walls and gaining strength.

In the left corner, a streak of red light zipped past me and joined with a blue one.

"It's working!" Chloe said as she squeezed my hand. "Everyone, keep going!"

We chanted louder, and the echoes grew more powerful. White and black streaks of light mixed with the red and blue. They circled around the ceiling until a gold dust appeared. It sprinkled into the other lights, and they glimmered.

Then the streaks of light bounced off the gem on the Buddha's forehead, revealing a mesmerizing rainbow.

"So beautiful!" I said.

The rainbow transformed into numbers: *35.0594, 126.9850.*

Chloe recognized them immediately. "Those are coordinates. Latitude and longitude."

I quickly typed the coordinates into the map on my phone and pressed enter. The location popped up right away.

"I got it," I said, waving my phone. "It's in Hwasun."

"Let's go eat now," Eugene said. "All that winning is exhausting."

"Maybe we can still make it today?" Chloe said.

Joon shook his head. "We should all rest."

"I agree," I chimed in. "Because what if there's another trial once we get there?" We'd be clobbered, in the state we were all in right now. A good night's sleep and some food would definitely help.

"That's true," Chloe said. "No chance we'd pass another trial."

Now that we were students at the school and on an IMA mission, we had access to all the safe houses. I scanned the ones listed on our document.

"Two options for the night," I said. "One is closer to here, and the other is closer to the train station."

Joon looked at his phone and said, "I vote for closest one."

"I don't even need to look," Eugene said. "Plus one for closest."

Chloe looked at the map. "The train station would be helpful, but we can just ride the bus tomorrow." She pointed to her phone. "The bus stops a couple of blocks from the closest safe house."

Finally we all agreed on something.

After a ten-minute cab ride, we arrived at Hwangridan-gil in Gyeongju, an area lined with hanok—traditional Korean homes—that had all been completely converted into restaurants, coffee shops, and stores. Even though it was almost nine p.m., the streets were bustling with people. The stores had all turned on their lanterns, which gave the area a warm, yellowish, mystical glow.

The navigation on my phone beeped and directed us to take a left at the corner.

"Should we stop somewhere to eat first?" Chloe asked.

"Home first," Joon said as he pointed to his leg. "It looks like I dipped my leg in ketchup."

Eugene lugged his bag. "Definitely home first."

I felt bad that no one ever really agreed with Chloe, but sometimes it seemed like she was in a world of her own. "According to the navigation, it should be here."

Right past a closed makeup store was a large stone wall with a wooden door. The gate was high, but I could still make out the beautiful winged roof of a hanok.

Chloe knocked on the door.

No one answered.

"Are you sure you entered the right location?" Joon asked.

Of course I had. It wasn't that complicated, just click on the address, and the navigation automatically directed us.

"Slip your IDs under the door," said a voice.

Once we did as we were told, an old woman with graying hair and wearing a flower-print dress opened the door. "You kids get younger every year. They sent me babies this time."

Eugene bowed and said, "With all due respect, we won the challenge at school fair and square."

She tapped his shoulder. "Ah, so much spark in you."

She held the door open for us, and we walked in onto a pebbled path lit up with paper lanterns hanging on poles. It led the way to a large hanok with sliding doors.

An old man in a dark blue sweater-vest greeted us.

"Welcome!" he said with a warm smile. "My wife and I have been hosting agents and agents in training for fifty years now."

"Wow," I said. "That's a long time."

"Yes," he said while opening the sliding door. "I wouldn't be surprised if all your parents stayed here at some point."

Surprisingly, the inside was a mixture of a modern interior with traditional architecture. The living room had a light gray sectional couch with colorful pillows. In the center of a marble coffee table was an orchid. Off to the side was a glass dining table with white chairs. The kitchen was completely modern and even prettier than the one in our house.

There were exposed wooden beams across the ceiling and along the walls, which contrasted well with the white walls, giving the room a more traditional hanok feel. Along the walls were sliding hanji doors decorated with wooden latticework.

The old woman pointed to the doors on either side of the living room. "We have two rooms on this side, and two on the other side."

"That's perfect," I said. After having a roommate at

school, I couldn't wait to sleep in a room all by myself.

"Dibs!" Eugene said as he sprinted to a room. Joon followed after him.

"I guess we're on this side," Chloe said.

"I'm good with that," I said, and linked arms with her.

The old woman said, "Put your bags down and come meet me in the yard." She pointed at the door behind the kitchen.

The bedroom had sliding panels for the windows, which looked like miniature doors. A brush painting of a cat and a butterfly hung on the wall across from a low bed covered with a crisp white blanket.

I plopped down on the bed and stared at the crisscrossed wooden beams on the ceiling. I hoped all safe houses were like this.

Before going outside, I quickly texted Umma. Just got to safe house in Gyeongju. Love it!

She immediately texted back, I'm so proud of you. Make sure you eat enough today and rest a lot. Don't forget to brush your teeth before bed. Be polite and respectful to your hosts. And make sure u make ur b in the morn. We believe in you. I love you so much!

I giggled and texted back. Okay, Umma. I love you too! Her text messages were always like an essay. And she abbreviated random things that literally no one else did, making it difficult to figure out what she was saying. She said it made her feel young, like how kids these days shorten everything. But by *make ur b in the morn*, I knew she meant *make your bed in the morning*.

We went out to the backyard after putting our stuff away. A large pine tree stood in the corner of the yard near the stone wall that surrounded the house. A large platform was in the center. In Western backyards, people sat on chairs and ate at a table. Traditionally in Korea, people ate on top of these large platforms at a low table, and then it was removed when the meal was finished. Which was pretty cool, because once you were done eating, you could also lie down and relax.

The old man walked out carrying a table full of food. "Watch out." He placed the rectangular wooden table on top of the platform. "Now it's ready."

There were gulbi (grilled yellow corvina fish), dwenjang-jjigae (bean paste soup with tofu), and bowls of rice. In round, shallow plates were side dishes called banchan. Umma always teased me that I ate all my banchan and meat first before even touching my rice.

"Now sit here," the old woman said. Heat lamps switched on, and a string of light bulbs swayed over our heads.

The table was the perfect height. When I sat down

with my legs crossed, everything was a little below chest level and easy to reach.

"Jalmeokgessumnida," Joon said as he sipped his water.

"Thank you for the delicious food," said Chloe.

I picked up my chopsticks and grabbed a piece of gim (seaweed), then placed it on top of my rice. I loved rice and seaweed. Best combo ever.

Now that we were relaxed, I realized that we hadn't checked in with the other team or IMA. Whoops!

"I'm going to check in now," I said.

"Go ahead," Joon said. "You're in charge of that."

I tapped on the Project HH app on my phone. At the prompt I entered our team name: Air Check. There was a button on the top right that said *Check in with IMA*. I clicked on it. Then another message appeared that read *Current location?* I typed in *Hwangridan-gil*. The final message said *Check in at next location*.

In the left-hand corner was a button labeled *Team Sonic Boom*. That must've been what the other team named themselves. I clicked on it, and it asked me to write updates and important information. I quickly wrote down everything that had happened so far and pressed send. Team Sonic Boom hadn't left a message for us yet, which probably meant that they were in the midst of their trial, and I didn't want them to feel pressured by leaving another message.

"What's that house over there?" I pointed to a smaller hanok on the other side of the yard.

"That's where we live," said the old man.

"I bet you have so many cool stories," said Eugene.

The old woman put some fish on top of our bowls. "Eat these, too."

"So many," said the old man. "But the most memorable one was when we met Warrior Ji."

We all gasped. He was more famous than a celebrity. So incredible. I wish I could've met him too and asked all my questions.

"Did he bring his cheonma?" I asked. Cheonma were reserved for the best of the best warriors. It was a special horse with wings on its feet. It was the Korean version of a pegasus. In mythology, the cheonma had eight legs, but from what I knew, the eight-legged ones were extinct. They'd evolved into four-legged ones.

"What did his sword look like?" Joon asked.

Eugene asked, "Was he as tall and strong as they say?"

"Which mission was it?" Chloe asked.

The old man chuckled and rubbed his hands together.

"Some details are classified, but I can tell you he was about a hundred ninety centimeters tall, muscular with rugged features, and humble. He had a heart of gold and was serious about protecting humanity."

We all nodded. That totally seemed like him. "What else can you tell us?" I asked.

"He did have a cheonma, which he called Byuli. They were the best of friends and always looked out for each other," the old man said. "I'm afraid I can't share what mission he was on, though."

"Well, I hope I get a cheonma someday," I said.

Everyone nodded in agreement. It would be the ultimate sign that we had made it as warriors.

"Thank you for the story and food," Joon said. "I'm so full."

The old man stood up to clear the table.

Eugene jumped up to help.

"It's okay, sit back down," said the old man. "I can do this very fast."

Eugene did as he was told.

The old woman gazed up at the night sky. "The prophecy says that a child born under the Bukduchilseong, the Big Dipper, will save us all. Traditionally, people studied and read the stars to tell fortunes."

"I don't see which constellation you're talking about," I said.

She chuckled. "All you young kids, forgetting the old ways."

Eugene craned his neck. "Those stars? Next to the big shiny one?"

"The big shiny one is Polaris," said Joon. "Not that one."

The old woman stood up and grinned. "Lie down and watch."

We all lay down on the platform. I pushed Joon's foot away from my face. "Can you please lie down the other way?"

He grunted and swiveled so his head was next to mine. "Better?"

The old woman stood in the middle of the yard and swished her finger in the air, then pointed at the sky.

Stars glimmered one by one.

"One, two, three, four, five, six, and seven," said the old woman. "Alkaid, Mizar, Alioth, Megrez, Dubhe, Merak, Phecda."

"You forgot one more," Chloe said.

Sure enough, an eighth star glimmered bright.

Chapter 17

"There are only supposed to be seven stars in this constellation." The old woman's eyebrows furrowed, and she walked back and forth nervously.

I sat up. "What does that mean, then?"

She shook her head gravely and tightened the shawl around her shoulders. "Oh, my dear. Do you see how close the eighth star is to the seventh?"

They were pretty close together. Just barely touching.

"That means," she continued, "that they are equals and there will be a battle for power."

Yikes! That sounded scary. But who believed in all this stuff anymore?

As if she'd read my mind, the old woman said, "This is all old mumbo jumbo." She quickly changed the subject. "My husband is probably sleeping, so let's go back to the guesthouse, and I'll show you a different type of fortune-telling that you are all probably more familiar with."

"Like tarot cards?" Joon said as he followed behind her.

Inside the kitchen, she poured water into an electric teakettle and took out four green celadon teacups from the cupboard.

Celadon was a form of pottery during the Goryeo dynasty, and it required very exact timing in the kiln to achieve a beautiful green hue. Halmoni loved anything made of celadon, so I knew all about the history of it. Also, back in California we had the special celadon vase of Nammo and Joonjeong fighting, until it broke because of the shadows.

The old woman opened a drawer and took out a jar with what looked like lavender or another leafy herb. Then she twisted open the lid of a bottle with a liquid that glowed a fluorescent blue. She squeezed a drop into each cup and then dropped a tea bag into each. Once the water was ready, she poured it into each cup.

"Here you go," she said, placing a teacup in front of each of us. "Don't drink it yet. It needs time to steep."

I wrapped my hands around the cup, and steam tickled my nose. Images of elegant white cranes soaring in between wispy clouds decorated the cup.

The old woman disappeared into a room that looked like an oversized pantry, with rows of herbs and unidentifiable objects in clear jars. On the opposite wall were shelves filled with books, trinkets, huge bone-stew boiling pots, and a container of large acupuncture needles.

Who were these people? These seemed like very strange items to have at home for people just hosting agents and agents in training overnight.

When she returned, she sat down in front of us with a traditional seonjang-bound book. This type of side-stitched bound book had been popular during the Joseon dynasty.

"What is the tea for?" I asked.

"For drinking, of course," she said. "It'll help warm up your body and help you have a good night's sleep."

She took out a blank piece of paper and pen. "Now go around and tell me your full names and birth dates."

"Is this saju?" Joon asked as he took a sip of tea.

Saju was the Korean version of tarot cards. I'd never had mine read before. Even though I didn't really believe in this stuff, I was curious to know what my future held. Hopefully nothing bad.

"Eugene Yang, January 8."

"Joon Kim, April 17."

"Chloe Shim, June 3."

"Lia Park, February 25."

"Don't you need our birth year?" I asked.

"I already know it," she said with a wink. "You're all twelve years old, right?"

"Ne," we said. Her math skills were on point.

She flipped open her book to a page written entirely in hanmun, Chinese characters that Koreans used before the invention of hangul, the Korean alphabet.

"Ask me something," she said. "Anything you want."

"Am I going to get straight A's?" Joon asked.

What a waste of a question.

"Ah, something most students want to know." She flipped through the pages of the seonjang book until she found one that started to glow.

With her finger, she traced something on the page. "I'm inputting your name and birth date."

Purple smoke rose up from the book and formed the hanja character for the word *effort*.

"It means that it'll depend on how much work you put into your studies," she explained.

"That's too easy," Eugene said. "I could've told him that."

She smiled mysteriously. "Why don't you ask me something more personal, then?"

Eugene thought for a moment and said, "Why don't I like Children's Day?"

She turned to a different page and traced his name and birth date. The hanja for *courage* appeared in purple smoke.

She spoke softly and held his hand over the table. "Something in your past hurt you, and it will require courage for you to overcome it."

Eugene looked a little surprised. He quickly withdrew his hand and didn't say anything more. I wondered what it could be that she was talking about. Maybe I'd ask him about it later.

"Well, I think we all want to know this," I said. "Will we get the heavenly heirlooms?"

She nodded approvingly. "Now you're asking the right kind of question."

"And maybe ask whether there's anything we should avoid?" I added.

"Are you the only team on this recovery mission?" she asked.

"No," Chloe said. "There's a second team bringing back the third heirloom."

"I will need their names and birth dates too," she said. "Because your fates are intertwined for the mission."

"We don't have them," Joon said.

I pulled out my phone and clicked on the Project HH app. Just like I'd thought, our full names and birth dates were listed under *Team Members*.

"I have them on here," I said, and handed her my phone.

"Nice save," Chloe said.

She flipped to a different page and traced all eight of our names and birth dates with her finger. When she was done, the hanmun letters already written on the page of the book lifted off it and bounced aggressively up and down. She frowned and stepped back. The letters grew bigger and bigger until they collided and exploded in the air.

Red smoke appeared and formed two different hanja characters.

The old woman's face froze, and she studied us carefully.

"What does it mean?" Chloe asked.

"Is it that bad?" I said.

The woman paused and said, "You are all in danger."

"Don't worry," Joon said. "We already passed the trial at the Seokguram."

"Not from trials," she said. "From each other."

"What are you talking about?" I asked. "Our teamwork was so great, we even beat the Guardian Kings at jokgu."

She pointed to the first character. "That means *betrayal*. There is a traitor among you." Then she pointed to the next character. "And the traitor will bring death."

I was stunned. No way that was possible. These were my friends. My best friends. I thought I knew them pretty well, and they just didn't have it in them to do something like that. There had to be a mistake.

"Maybe it's Joon," Eugene said. "He totally betrayed us earlier."

Joon turned red and said, "But I apologized. I thought we were all good now."

"Well, she said 'baeshinja,'" said Chloe. "And you're the only one who did that."

"Stop it," I said. "It's not fact. No one can tell our future, right?"

"The future is unwritten," the old woman said slowly. "But it's a fine line, because we believe in destiny."

"Can you please tell them it's not me?" Joon said.

She held his hand. "I'm sorry. I can't do that."

"Wait," I said. "But didn't you read the fortune for both teams at the same time?"

"I did," she said gravely. "This fortune applies to all eight of you."

I felt a little relief that it probably meant the traitor was someone on the other team.

"I can think of one particular person on the other team who fits this role perfectly," Eugene said.

Of course. Who else could it be? No one was meaner than Victor. I cringed, thinking back to when he'd had a choke hold on me during the tuho game.

"It's got to be Victor," Chloe said.

"It's not him," Joon protested. "I see him all the time in our house, and he wouldn't do that."

"Why not?" Eugene asked. "He seems pretty capable of a lot of things."

"Because he really wanted to go on this mission."

"Probably to sabotage us," I said.

"That doesn't make sense," Joon said. "Why would he want to do that when everything is at stake if we fail?"

I was mad that Joon was defending him but also that his reasoning seemed very rational. Why would any of us want to sabotage this mission? I was pretty sure no one was looking forward to dying or being plunged into darkness forever.

"It's probably someone on the other team?" I asked the old woman.

"No, I didn't say that." She pointed at the letters still suspended in the air. "I don't know who it is. But when a fortune has red letters, it's usually a warning that something bad will happen, so you can prepare for it."

"That just sounds so horrible," said Chloe.

"How are we supposed to finish our mission?" asked Eugene.

Exactly what I was thinking. I wished we had never agreed to do this fortune-telling saju reading. In some ways, maybe ignorance was bliss, if knowing was going to change how we worked together to recover the heavenly heirloom.

The woman looked at the clock and said, "Oh my goodness, I've kept you too long."

Joon stood up to clear the table.

The old woman shooed us away. "I'll take care of it. Go and rest."

We all bowed and said, "Annyeonghuijumuseyo."

"Good night," said Joon.

She waved, but I couldn't help noticing the scared look in her eyes.

The next morning, after a hearty breakfast, we rode the bus to Hwasun in complete silence. It was the last stop. Chloe played a game on her phone, while Eugene and Joon were fast asleep.

Everything the old woman had said last night replayed on an infinite loop in my head. I refused to accept that there was a baeshinja among us and that one of us would die. Or was it that there would just be death? Whose death? Maybe the King of Darkness. The thing with these fortunes was that they were never crystal clear.

Which was why focusing on who the traitor might be would be useless. It would just break us apart. And maybe if there was a traitor, we could turn the traitor back to our side.

I must've dozed off, because when I woke up, the bus was pulling into a large parking lot. Where were we?

"Ajeossi, yeogi eodieyo?" I asked.

"Hwasunae dochakhaessumnida," he answered.

"Wake up," I said as I shook Eugene. "We're here at Hwasun."

Eugene yawned and stretched his arms. "That was so fast."

"No, sleeping beauty," I said. "It was a five-hour ride."

Joon and Chloe woke up too. "Where are we?" Chloe asked.

We got off the bus. "The ajeossi said this was Hwasun, but I think we have to walk from here," I said.

A large bamboo forest stretched out behind the parking lot.

"Why do I get the feeling we have to go through there?" Joon said, pointing at the enormous bamboos.

"Designated navigator," Eugene teased. "Where to?"

I laughed out loud and flashed my phone to everyone. "Actually, I've been tracking it since the bus ride." I pointed to the bamboo forest. "Joon is right. We have to go through there."

"Why am I not surprised?" Chloe said with a groan.

The bamboo was really thick and very tall. I remembered Halmoni saying that bamboo was actually an invasive species, and if you weren't careful, it could take over the entire garden. Because a bamboo's roots could grow up to twenty feet sideways. This bamboo forest had definitely taken over a massive piece of land.

"I don't see an end to this forest," said Joon.

I checked my navigation. "It's a little farther."

There wasn't a clear path, and so we walked around between the bamboo trees. A couple of minutes later, I saw the last row of bamboo trees and a green field just beyond it.

"We're almost there!" I said.

Chloe said, "Never been so happy to see grass."

Joon looked at Eugene and said, "Race you?"

"Go!" Eugene said as he took off.

"Cheater!" Joon shouted after him. "Do-over!"

Chloe and I laughed and joined them.

As he was running, Joon tripped over a tree branch and fell flat on his face. He groaned and sat up. Next to him was a large egg that had been buried under some fallen leaves.

"What's an egg doing in the middle of a forest?" Eugene squatted down to get a closer look.

"Run!" I said. "It's going to turn into the dalgyal gwishin!"

Joon and Eugene bolted up and backed away.

The egg rustled and then levitated.

It was too late to run now.

"Don't look at it!" I squeezed my eyes shut and yanked my fan out from my holster and flicked it open. I gripped the hilt of the sword and immediately swung it as hard as I could. But I wasn't hitting anything. Something brushed past my arm, sending chills up my body.

"Circle formation," I yelled, and reached out my hand until I felt another hand.

"It's me," Joon said. "I have Eugene."

Eugene shouted, "Chloe, where are you?"

"Here," she said, and gripped my wrist.

"Backs against each other," I commanded. "And no matter what, do not open your eyes. If you look directly at it, you will die."

I moved backward, one foot behind the other, until I felt someone's back. "Eugene?"

"Yeah," he said. "Confirm formation!"

We all shouted, "Confirm!"

"Weapons out!"

I couldn't see, but I heard the clicking sound of the fans opening.

"Swing your weapons," I said.

I jabbed my sword and waved it in front of me. Where was the egg ghost?

"I've got nothing," said Joon.

I peeked my eyes open and focused on the ground. Nothing.

This was our chance to get as far away as we could.

"Eugene," I said. "Look down and get us out of here."

"It's not in front of me," he said. "I'm going."

He dragged us forward one step at a time. I kept my eyes glued to the ground.

From the corner of my eye, I spotted the hem of a white hanbok coming toward me. "It's here!"

Eugene suddenly darted forward without telling us what he was doing, and I tumbled onto my back. I closed my eyes and flipped over onto my stomach.

"Lia!" Chloe called out.

"I'm on the ground!" I clutched my sword and swung it in front of me, which only rustled the leaves. I squinted and spotted the bottom of the white hanbok drawing closer. Then it disappeared.

"Keep your eyes closed," Chloe yelled.

Her voice sounded close by.

Something whooshed over my head, and I heard a sickening crack.

"You can get up now." Chloe grabbed my arm.

"Are you sure?" I got up but couldn't open my eyes. What if it came back?

She linked arms with me. "I killed it."

I opened my eyes and stared at her. "How? Where is it?"

Chloe had on these huge goggles with blacked-out lenses. "What are those, Chloe?"

"It floated into the air and turned upside down so it could kill you."

Behind me, Chloe's spear had shattered the dalgyal gwishin's egg-shaped face into tiny pieces. The white hanbok lay on the ground, lifeless.

"How did you know that would kill it?" I shuddered, thinking of what might have happened.

She shrugged. "I didn't, but I had to do something."

"But you can't see," I said.

She patted her goggles. "Actually, with these I can sense heat and cold. And ghosts are cold."

"You're a genius!" I hugged her tightly. "Thank you for saving my life, Chloe."

Chapter 18

"I thought you were right next to me," Joon said with a worried look on his face.

"It's okay," I said. "I'm fine." In any other situation, I would've been so angry that Joon and Eugene had run off without checking on the rest of the team, but given that they'd had their eyes shut, I let it go. Besides, I was thrilled that we had all gotten out of there alive.

I caught them up on how Chloe had saved the day.

"Way to go, Chloe," Eugene said, and gave her a high five.

She blushed. "Any of you would have done that for me."

"You're still a superstar," I said.

"Okay, I'll take that." She grinned.

The phone in my pocket beeped. I had forgotten that the navigation was still on.

"Where to?" Joon pointed to three small hills.

I ran ahead to the left one. "It should be just over this hill."

At the top I stopped in my tracks. Massive rocks of different shapes were everywhere, spaced out randomly.

"Whoa," Joon said, standing next to me. "Where are we?"

I couldn't believe I hadn't put it together. Totally made sense, considering what city we were in. "We're in Hwasun, at one of the most popular goindol sites. This dolmen site is so famous that it's designated as National Historic Site Number 410."

"Are you sure?" Eugene said. "Looks like a lot of big rocks."

"Lia is a walking textbook," Joon said. "She's usually right."

"Usually?" I joked. "I'm always right about these things."

"O Great Search Engine," said Eugene with his hands pressed together in front of him. "Please enlighten us."

Chloe rolled her eyes and said, "Cut it out. I think it's cool that Lia knows all about these things."

"Thanks, Chloe," I said. But I wasn't really offended. Before IMS, I'd resented having to study Korean history while Joon learned magic, but now I thought of it as my second superpower.

Knowledge was power.

"The Hwasun goindol are from the Korean Bronze Age, which was around 1000 BC."

"Kind of reminds me of Stonehenge," said Joon.

I knew Joon would get it. "These are dolmens too. And did you know that Korea has more than thirty-five thousand?"

"Amazing that there are so many on this tiny peninsula," said Chloe.

"Right?" I said. "That's forty percent of the entire world's dolmens! That's why the Gochang, Hwasun, and Ganghwa dolmen sites have also been designated as a World Heritage Site by UNESCO."

"Wait," said Eugene. "Aren't dolmens graves?"

All around us were megaliths that towered over us. "We're standing in the middle of a cemetery," I said.

Chloe clung to me and hid her face behind my back. "Graveyards give me the creeps."

"These are massive." Joon walked around a large rock. "How tall do you think they are?"

"Sixteen to twenty-two feet tall." I was pretty impressed that I knew that.

"So which rock are we looking for?" said Chloe.

I looked down at my navigation, which hadn't ended, and kept walking until I saw a small dirt path on the right, hidden by low-hanging branches of trees. I was relieved it wasn't another bamboo forest where a dalgyal gwishin might live. "This way."

I ducked under the branches and couldn't believe my eyes. Standing in front of me was an enormous rock with a very distinctive inscription carved into it.

"This is the Pingmae Bawi," I said. "It's a capstone dolmen. Big rock on top of tiny ones."

"How can you tell?" Eugene said. "They all look the same."

"All pretty unique, actually." I pointed to the rectangular carving on the rock. "The Pingmae Bawi has this on it. It says 'property of the Min family.'"

"Oh, I remember reading about that," Joon said. "The Min family carved it into this rock, not knowing it was a dolmen, to mark the boundaries of their land."

"That's great and all," said Chloe. "But is there anything in your brain database about how to find the heavenly heirloom?"

Eugene grabbed the bottom of the rock and grunted.

I laughed. "No way you're going to be able to lift

that up," I said. "It's almost three hundred tons."

"That's like more than a hundred cars," Chloe said.

"I know that," Eugene said. "I just wanted to see how heavy it was."

Joon scrolled down on his phone. "The document doesn't say anything specific. Just says to use our Obangsaek ui him to locate the heavenly heirloom."

"Let's try it," Chloe said. "It worked at the Seokguram Grotto."

"Maybe we were given general directions on purpose, since no one's supposed to know the locations." I reached for Eugene's and Chloe's hands.

We stood in a circle and chanted, "Obangsaek ui him" over and over again. After the tenth time, red, blue, white, and black beams of light shot out from our hands. They wrapped around the Pingmae Bawi. A gold beam rose from the ground inside our circle and soared to the goindol. It weaved over and under the other colors, creating a net.

Then the unexpected happened.

The massive twenty-two-foot-tall megalith floated up. It didn't stop until it was a speck in the air. In the spot where it had stood was an entryway surrounded by small rocks.

I inched closer to get a better look at what was down there. The ground rumbled, and I saw two beady red eyes glaring up at me.

I yelled and ran back to my friends. "There's something in there!"

Slime oozed out of the hole, and something growled as it slowly emerged and began to take shape. The eyes traveled up to the top of the slime blob and fixed their gaze on us. The top and bottom stretched out toward us. We moved back to avoid getting caught in gushing slime. It sprouted large pointy teeth like a shark's and morphed into a giant open mouth with those menacing red eyes.

"What in the world is that?" Eugene whispered.

The creature said in a low voice, without moving its mouth, "I am the Geogugwi."

I'd only read about this monster in my textbooks, and even they didn't have much information. But I could see why IMA had chosen the Geogugwi to protect a heavenly heirloom.

"What is it that you seek?" The voice shook the ground, and more slime oozed out of its open mouth, like saliva.

"We have to retrieve the heavenly heirloom," I said.

"Answer this, and what you seek shall be found," it

said. "What can work until the day it dies, but its life's work can be destroyed in a second?"

"I hate riddles," Eugene grumbled.

"That's irrelevant," Chloe said. "Think!"

She was right. Whether we liked it or not, we had no choice but to answer the riddle. But I was completely stumped.

"How about an ant?" said Joon. "It's alive and works hard."

"That totally makes sense," Eugene said. "And anthills can be destroyed really quickly."

Before I could stop him, Joon blurted out, "An ant."

The Geogugwi opened its mouth even wider, and a slimy tongue oozed out. It came straight for Joon and wrapped around his feet.

"Help!" Joon fell face-forward to the ground as the tongue dragged him inside the Geogugwi's mouth.

I lunged to grab his arm, but I was too late. The Geogugwi swallowed Joon and opened its mouth again.

"No!" I shouted. Chloe and Eugene pulled me back.

"Answer wrong and pay the price," bellowed the Geogugwi.

"If we solve your riddle," I said, "can you give us back our friend?"

"Two more chances. Answer right, and treasures you shall receive."

We had to get Joon back.

"I can't lose him," I said.

Eugene hugged me. "He's our friend too. We'll rescue him no matter what."

"Think," Chloe urged. "What else could it be?"

So it wasn't an ant. What else worked until it died? "Maybe the word 'worked' isn't so literal."

"That's true," Eugene said. "That's the thing I hate about riddles, because they're not straightforward."

"What else could 'work' mean?" Chloe said.

I brainstormed out loud. "Books and paintings can be 'bodies of work.'"

"And a book can be burned and destroyed," Eugene said. "And when it's fully written, then it dies, because there are no more pages to write on."

I faced the Geogugwi. "We have the answer. It's—"

"A book," Eugene said, and then turned to me. "If I'm wrong, you can rescue me and Joon."

He'd barely finished his sentence when the slimy tongue slithered out of the Geogugwi's mouth again and wrapped around Eugene's ankle. The Geogugwi yanked Eugene into its mouth.

I dropped to the ground and felt my panic. Two of my friends had been taken, and I had absolutely no clue what the answer was. We had only one shot left to rescue them or they'd be lost forever. Who knew what the Geogugwi would do to them? A wrong answer could mean that Chloe or I would get taken. And I couldn't let that happen. I owed her big-time.

Chloe sat down next to me. "Lia, you need to focus."

"How can I when they're gone?" I said, looking at her stoic face. "We could be next, you know."

"Because they're depending on us to solve the riddle and get the heavenly heirloom."

She was right. And if we got the right answer, we'd get everything back.

"I think we were on the right track, though," said Chloe. "It's not the verb 'work.'"

"What are some things that are connected to 'work'?" I asked. "Word associations."

"With painting," she said, "there's canvas, brush, oil, pastels, shows, museums, curator."

"For books, there's paper, chapters, writing, computer, printer, pen, pencil, words," I added.

Then it hit me.

I knew the answer. It had to be this.

"It's a pencil," I said.

Chloe didn't answer and looked deep in thought. "Explain."

"Because a pencil can write or work until it's a stub," I said.

"Why not a pen, then?" she asked. "It can write until it runs out."

I jumped up and down because now I was even more sure that I had the right answer. Everything fit. "Because with a pen, you can't erase what you wrote, but you can use an eraser to undo everything that's written with a pencil."

She grinned. "I think you're right!"

I faced the Geogugwi and tried to avoid looking into its mouth. "The answer is a pencil."

With a squelch the Geogugwi turned into a mound of slime and drained into the hole. In its place stood a little boy. His hair was in two little buns on the top of his head, and he wore white pants and a long green tunic with gold decoration along the neck and sleeves. In his hands he held a tray covered with a blue cloth.

"Who are you?" I demanded. "Where are my friends?"

He smiled and said, "I'm Dongja. You passed the test."

"Where's the heavenly heirloom?" Chloe asked.

Dongja pushed the tray toward me. "Please lift up the cloth."

His voice was so soothing, and he had such a happy face that I couldn't help but be a little wary of his cheery demeanor after almost getting eaten alive. I lifted the blue cloth up, and a rattle appeared.

We'd done it! My hands shook as I picked up the rattle. I couldn't believe we had successfully completed our first mission. And we were just First Years!

I passed it to Chloe, who held it carefully.

"And Joon and Eugene?" I asked. They were nowhere in sight.

Dongja clapped his hands twice, and they appeared in front of us. "I keep my promises."

I ran to hug them. "Are you two okay?"

Eugene patted his face and legs. "Whoa. That was the strangest experience."

"We were floating in this weird way," said Joon. "Completely surrounded by goo but not wet."

"I'm just glad you two weren't hurt," I said.

"Did you get the heavenly heirloom?" Joon asked.

Chloe passed it over to him. "Here it is."

They all took a turn holding it. The rattle looked really old and didn't feel like it had any magic in it. Eugene handed it to me. I wrapped it up carefully and put it in my bag.

"I can take you where you need to go," Dongja said. "Unless you want to wait for the next bus."

"That would be wonderful," I said.

Joon typed something on his phone. "We should let IMA know that we got the heavenly heirloom."

"Are you contacting IMA?" I asked.

"No," he said. "Just writing some notes."

Our phones beeped at the same time. It was a message from IMA that said, *Report to Green Rose Hotel at Wolchulsan Peak No. 2 immediately.*

"I guess this is where we're headed," I said.

Dongja looked at the address and said, "Ready?"

Then he clapped his hands four times.

CHAPTER 19

When I opened my eyes, we were standing in the middle of a hotel lobby. Even though we'd just appeared out of thin air, no one paid any attention to us.

To our left was a convenience store and a restaurant.

"I'm starving," Joon said.

My stomach grumbled. "Should we pick up something at the convenience store?"

"Yes, please," Chloe said.

We practically skipped to the store. Along the walls were all the refrigerated foods and beverages. In the center of the store were just two aisles of chips, cookies, and other snacks.

I walked around and finally settled on three rolls of tuna kimbap, two bottles of orange juice, and a bag of gummy bears.

By the time I got to the cashier, everyone else had just finished checking out.

"What did you all get?" I asked as I put my items on the counter.

"Ramen, kimbap, some chips and drinks," Chloe said.

"Five rolls of tuna kimbap, and drinks," said Joon.

"Tuna sandwich, egg sandwich, bulgogi kimbap, chips, and drinks," Eugene said.

The cashier rung up my items. "Twenty thousand won," he said.

Good thing we always carried a little bit of extra cash in our backpacks for emergencies. I took the two green ten-thousand-won bills and handed them to him.

"I got kimbap too," I said.

We walked to the front desk to get our keys.

I stood at the counter with Joon while Eugene and Chloe sat on some chairs nearby and fiddled with their phones.

"Checking in?" said the man at the front desk.

"Yes," I said.

"Whose name would the reservation be under?" he said as he typed on his computer.

We pulled out our identification cards and placed them on the counter. "Maybe under Lia, Joon, Eugene, or Chloe?" I really hoped IMA had sent our names in.

"Your rooms are taken care of." He checked the IDs before sliding them back to us, along with four large, old-fashioned keys. "Rooms 301, 302, 303, and 305."

A message dinged on his computer screen. He looked up and studied my face carefully. "And remember, this is a sanctuary. Any kind of violence will not be tolerated."

Joon slipped his ID into his pocket. I smiled and took the keys. Then we speed-walked to the elevator. Chloe and Eugene followed behind us. Once I could no longer see the man at the front desk, I lowered my voice and asked the others, "What kind of hotel is this?"

A young woman with a small suitcase walked out of the elevator. She stopped to stare at her phone and then glared at us with red beady eyes. When she finally walked away, we could see that she had nine gray tails. Gumiho. A nine-tailed fox. Were we in a monster hotel? Is that why people were staring us down?

We hurried into the elevator. The number four was

missing from the panel because it was bad luck and meant death. I pressed three and waited for the doors to shut.

Once we were alone, Eugene said, "The sanctuary hotels are kind of like a neutral zone."

"Between people with magic and monsters?" I asked.

"Yeah," Joon said, "I've heard my dad mention places like this."

"Just fighting will get you banned from here," explained Eugene.

"And killing will get you banned from all sanctuaries," added Joon.

"Did you notice people staring at us?" I asked.

"Probably because we're human and minors," Chloe said. "Kids don't really come here alone."

The elevator door beeped and opened. On the wall, where there would usually be signs with ranges of numbers directing people to go left or right, there was a large grandfather clock.

I walked down the hallway and saw that none of the rooms had numbers on them.

"You won't find our rooms like that." Chloe stuck out her hand. "Key, please."

I passed one of the large brass keys to her. "How, then?"

She opened the front door of the clock. "What floor are we on again?"

"Third," I said.

Chloe turned the big hand counterclockwise three times. Then she slid the key into the hole above the number six and turned it.

A door halfway down the hallway beeped and swung open.

"How is that room 301?" I asked. It was a room smack in the middle of the hallway.

"For protection," Eugene said. "The rooms change locations every six hours, but of course you won't feel them moving."

"It's one of the reasons why this place is in high demand, and no one really breaks the rules," Joon added.

If I was on the run, this would definitely be on the top of my hideout list.

"Why don't you take that room?" Chloe said, handing me back the key. "I know you're super curious to see what it looks like."

Normally that would have been true, but I thought it was a little strange how everyone else knew so much about sanctuary hotels, almost as if they'd been here before.

"How do you all know so much?" I asked.

"After my dad let it slip about this place, I grilled him for days to get all the details," Joon said. "I can't believe you of all people didn't know about the sanctuaries."

"Well, they're not really advertised in books, since they're a secret," I said defensively. "So how would I know?"

Also, let's not forget the fact that my overprotective parents had shielded me from pretty much all the really cool aspects of IMA, for—as it turned out—good reasons.

"What about you, Eugene?" Joon said. "You seem to know your way around here."

He had a sad look on his face and spoke in a low voice. "My mom said that the last time anyone saw my dad was at this place."

I didn't know what to say except, "I'm so sorry." How horrible it must have been for him to be back here. All the memories.

"It's okay," Eugene said. "My mom's back home in France with her family. He's been missing for so long now. She couldn't bear to watch me go down the same path he did."

"That's so rough. I didn't know," Joon said.

"It's fine," Eugene said. "It's not something I broadcast everywhere I go."

"Can you tell us about your dad?" Chloe asked.

"You know, I really don't know that much about him," Eugene said, and changed the subject. "Chloe, have you been here before?"

"Actually, I have, with my parents a few times," she said. "I think we should go put our stuff down."

"Okay," I said. "We still have to check in with IMA, so meet in my room in ten minutes?"

"Make it thirty," Eugene said. "We all need to eat."

"Okay." I handed Chloe the three remaining keys and walked down the hallway to the open door.

Inside the room was a two-person sofa next to the window and a large table pressed against a wall. Above the king-size bed was a painting in a picture frame. I tugged on it, but it wouldn't budge. This seemed like the obvious location to put a safe. I ran my hand over the painting, and without warning, it dissolved, revealing a safe tucked away behind it.

I opened the safe and read the directions pasted inside. *Place all weapons and valuables inside. To open and close safe, deposit blood, and enter passcode.*

Ick. I hated needles, but it was a good security setup, because fresh blood and a passcode were really hard to fake.

They were very serious about this being a safe place. The rattle would definitely be considered a valuable. Then, of course, there was my fan. Even though it was disengaged now, I was pretty sure it counted as a weapon. After I placed them both inside, the safe said, "Weapon and valuable detected." I closed the door, and a needle popped out. I scrunched my face and placed my finger near it. The needle shot out and jabbed my finger. I yelped in pain and watched the needle and a huge drop of my blood disappear. The safe then said, "Blood deposited. Enter passcode." I punched in my favorite combination of numbers, 3790. There was a clicking sound, and the safe disappeared into the wall and was replaced by a different picture.

From the window, I could see the tops of different mountain peaks. The hotel was on one of the lower peaks and looked over a cliff. It was mostly surrounded by trees, a good idea so that a random no-magic hiker couldn't stumble upon it.

I took out my tuna kimbap and unwrapped it. It had perilla leaves, tuna, radishes, and carrots inside. I popped one into my mouth, and surprisingly it was pretty decent for convenience store pre-made food.

I pressed the number one on my phone and heard

the phone ringing. I couldn't wait to tell Umma about my day.

Umma answered the phone. "Yeoboseyo."

"Hello, guess who?" I said as I switched on my camera.

"Aigoo. Uri gangaji sugohaesseo," said Umma.

Gangaji was a term of endearment in Korean that meant *puppy*. I'd never understood it, but it still felt comforting to hear her call me.

"Where are you?" Even though she was holding the phone up close to her face, I could see from the background that she wasn't at home.

"Nundo johtah. Umma chingu jipe wasseo."

I definitely had a sharp sense for these things. And she never hung out at anyone's house.

"Chingu nugu?" I asked.

"You don't know my friend," she said, and quickly changed the subject. "Where's everyone else?"

"They went to change," I said. "They should be here soon, though, so we can report to IMA."

"Lia, listen very carefully," she said urgently. "We've been tracking the eighth human identity of the King of Darkness."

"Have you found it?"

"We narrowed it down," she whispered. "To someone at your school."

No way. It didn't make sense. How had the monster even gotten into someone at the school? I thought it was one of the most secure places ever. I got chills thinking that I might've passed by the monster and not even known it.

"Who is it?" I asked. "Is it a teacher? Administrator? Student?"

"We don't know yet," she said. "But don't tell your friends."

But this was major news, and I had to warn them too. "Why not?"

"Because you can't rule anyone out yet," she said. "Ummarang yaksokhae."

I paused. "Okay, I promise you, Umma."

There was a knock on my door.

"Who is that?" Umma whispered.

"Probably my friends," I said.

"Remember, don't tell them about the King of Darkness," she warned. "Even Joon."

Even though I didn't want to believe her suspicions, Umma was right. If the human identity of the King of Darkness was truly someone at our school, I couldn't rule anyone out. I needed to act like I knew nothing and try to figure it out myself first. I needed to collect evidence.

"Saranghae uri ttal," she said.

"I love you too, Umma," I said, and hung up the phone.

I rushed over to the door and looked out through the peephole. Joon, Chloe, and Eugene were standing by the door and chatting. I opened the door for them, and they barged in.

"What took you so long?" Chloe complained.

"My mom wanted to know how everything went," I said, and yawned. I hated lying to them, but I needed time to figure things out first.

"Let's hurry up and call IMA," Eugene said as he sat down on a chair.

I opened the Project HH app on my phone and pressed call. I put it on speaker, and we all gathered around the table.

Chloe sat down next to me and rested her head on her folded arm.

"Team Air Check, everyone safe?" Ms. Shin asked.

"Yes," I said. "We're all here at the sanctuary."

"Good," she said. "Mission status?"

The line crackled.

"We secured the heavenly heirloom," Joon said.

"That is amazing news," she said excitedly. "I always knew you kids could do it."

"Thank you," we said.

"Where's Team Sonic Boom?" I asked. They hadn't checked in or responded to my last message, and I was getting kind of worried.

"They had some issues," she said. "But it looks like they are back on track to recover the heirloom."

Now that I knew they were all right, I could feel a little gleeful sense of pride because they hadn't completed the mission successfully yet. We'd totally decimated them. I knew I shouldn't think of this as a competition, because we all had the same goals, but it felt so good to beat Victor. Maybe he was the eighth identity of the King of Darkness. Let's just say that if he was, I would not be surprised at all.

"Since your team is the closest, I have a new mission for you."

"We're ready," said Eugene.

"Cross the Gureumdari bridge . . . bring back the liquids."

Her voice cut in and out, and we couldn't make out the rest.

"What liquids?" I asked.

"To kill . . ." And then the call ended.

"Call her back!" Joon said.

"I'm trying!" But every time I pressed the call button, there was a busy signal.

"Let me try on my phone," Chloe said. She held the phone up to her ear and then shook her head. "Not answering."

Eugene looked at his watch and walked to the door. "Something must've happened to the connection. Let's keep trying on our own."

I pulled out my walkie-talkie. "Whoever gets through first can let everyone else know by using this."

"Great plan," Chloe said. "Can I please go rest now?"

Joon opened the door, and everyone filed out.

I closed the door behind them. I grabbed a towel from the bathroom and stuffed it under the door so they wouldn't see my feet as I looked through the peephole. The last thing I wanted was for them to think I didn't trust them. Eugene went straight to his room. But came back out a few seconds later wearing a baseball cap and gloves, which was strange, because it wasn't cold at all outside. He turned left to where the elevators were. Where could he be going? Why wasn't he going back to his room? We were on a mountain peak, so it wasn't like there was anything to do around here.

Joon went to his room, which was three doors down from mine, and picked something up from the floor before going in. Did someone else other than those at IMA headquarters know that we were here? Maybe Joon had texted Victor to let him know where we were. That would mean Joon was the weak link in our group. Then there was Chloe. She walked down to the end of the hall and looked around both ways before opening her door. Her body language looked like she was expecting to run into someone here. Who could it be that she was trying to hide from?

It was hard not to be suspicious of everything and everyone after hearing the new information from Umma. Maybe I was reading into too many things and letting my imagination run wild.

I doubted Joon would be able to fool me. If a monster was inside him, I was sure I'd see right through the disguise, and call him out for being an imposter. I thought back to everything that had happened with Eugene or Chloe and tried to remember anything off. But any strange behavior could've just been stress or a bad moment. After all the time we'd spent together, there'd be no way to hide something as major as being the actual King of Darkness. Right?

But the old woman had also said that there was a traitor among us. At the time, I'd thought she was referring to Victor, but I wasn't so sure anymore. And was it one traitor and one eighth identity of the King of Darkness? Or were both the same person?

The old woman's message could have been a premonition too, that one of us would betray the others at some point in time. Or had the potential to. And the other hanja character could have meant that death was something we would face. We were technically risking our lives on this mission to recover the heavenly heirlooms, because the trials were a do-or-die type of thing. If what Umma had said was true, and the eighth identity was a person at school, then all the kids and teachers were in danger.

Or it was one of *us*.

CHAPTER 20

Alarms blared and I woke up to red and blue lights flashing in my room. I must've fallen asleep. The bed vibrated as if there was a low-grade earthquake, while the painting flickered above my head. I ran my hand frantically over the painting. As soon as it faded away completely, the safe appeared, along with a needle. I winced as it poked my finger, but I fought through the pain and quickly entered my passcode. The safe whirred open. I stuffed the rattle and fan into my bag and ran toward the door, which was wide open.

The emergency fire sprinklers turned on, spraying everywhere. All the doors were open, and people were rushing down the hallway toward the emergency staircase. I spotted Joon running toward me.

"What's going on?" I yelled as I wiped water off my face.

"We've got to get out of here," he said, pulling my hand.

"Is there a fire?"

The floor rumbled and began to cave as the row of rooms on the right slowly tilted toward me.

"There's been an attack." He ran in the opposite direction from where everyone else was headed. "We need to get out of here."

"We're going the wrong way," I yelled.

He stopped and looked me straight in the eye. "You have to trust me. I'll explain later."

"Fine," I said. He looked so serious. "What about the others?"

"No one's after them," he said. "They've probably already evacuated."

I yanked my hand out of his grasp. "I don't care. We don't leave our friends behind."

I pulled the walkie-talkie from my bag, pressed the button on the side, and held it to my mouth. "Eugene! Chloe!"

A man in a bulky jacket slowed down as he ran toward

us. He stopped in front of us and checked something on his phone. Then he looked us up and down.

"Are you Lia Park?" he asked me.

"Yes," I said.

"No, that's not her," Joon said.

"Well, if it isn't my lucky payday," sneered the man, walking menacingly toward us.

I stuffed the walkie-talkie into my back pocket, pulled out my fan, and unclasped it.

"What do you want?" I demanded with my sword out in front of me.

Joon unclasped his fan and aimed his bow at the man.

The man pulled a large ax from under his jacket. "If you come nicely," he said to me, "I won't kill you."

"I'm a really good shot," Joon said. "You leave now, and I won't kill *you*."

What was Joon doing?

I pushed Joon back and swung my sword. "Just go. There's two of us and one of you."

"You babies think you can beat me?" he said, and snickered. "And besides, I'm not losing out on one billion won."

What? One billion won? For what?

Before I could even react, Joon shot an arrow and hit

the man in the thigh. He shouted in pain and lunged at us with his ax.

I stepped in front of Joon and slashed my sword across the man's arm.

"Run," I shouted to Joon.

We raced down the hall, and I yelled into the walkie-talkie. "Eugene! Chloe!"

Eugene's voice crackled through the walkie-talkie. "I'm here! In my room!"

"We're coming!" I shouted back.

When we got to Eugene's room, we saw Eugene sitting on the floor, with his feet caught in some electrical cords. "Help!"

I rushed over to him. "Are you hurt?"

Water dripped off his baseball cap. He struggled to loosen the cords with his gloved hands. "No, but I'm stuck!"

A large sofa covered an electrical socket, and the cords were tangled around the wooden legs, making it impossible for him to free himself. The more he tugged at the cords, the more they seemed to tighten around his ankles.

Joon and I grabbed different ends of the sofa and tried to pull it away from the socket. My hands slipped.

Everything was so wet because of the water from the sprinklers. The room tilted down even more, so the sofa was pressed solidly against the wall and refused to even budge.

"Scissors?" Joon asked. "Or Swiss Army knife things?"

What? Did he think I carried every random item? A knife wasn't so random for a mission, but I'd had to prioritize the space in my bag and had chosen not to bring a pocketknife, because I had a sword.

"I have my sword." I lifted my hands up and felt the water from the sprinklers pouring down. "But everything is wet. We can't chop an electrical cord."

Eugene yanked at the cord. "It's useless."

There was a loud crunch as the walls began to move.

"Get the heirloom out of here," Eugene said, putting on a brave face. "The sanctuary is in self-destruct mode."

"Not a chance." There was no way I was going to leave Eugene behind. I knew there had to be something else we could try. *Think, Lia!* I racked my brain for spells that I knew.

"Puleojigeora!" I chanted. Maybe if I could loosen the cords, untangle them just a little, it would be enough for Eugene to get his feet out.

The painting over Eugene's bed fell, and with a crack, the headboard of the bed broke.

"It's not working!" Joon yelled. "Try harder!"

I chanted again and again while Joon held on to the cords.

"I can feel them getting looser," Eugene shouted.

Joon yanked off Eugene's shoes. "Try wiggling your feet out!"

Eugene grunted and used both his hands to pull one foot out and then the other.

He stuffed his feet back into his sneakers and hugged me. "I owe you one."

The walls crashed down onto the door, leaving a triangle-shaped exit.

"Come on," I yelled as I ran and squeezed through the doorway.

The halls were almost empty except for a few stragglers who were running out of their collapsing rooms.

"Chloe!" I yelled.

Someone in a hooded raincoat that reached to the floor turned around. "Lia?"

It was Chloe's voice! She ran toward us. "I looked everywhere for you all!"

"Hug later," Joon shouted. "We're almost out of time."

"A part of that staircase at the other end of the hall is missing now," Chloe said.

The ceiling cracked, and the walls of the hallway began to cave in.

Joon sprinted down the hallway, counting rooms, until he stopped in front of one. "Found it."

We ran after him but kept falling down because everything was spinning. Bits of the ceiling crumbled down around us. Joon stood inside the room, in front of a giant hole in the floor.

"What is this?" I asked. I couldn't believe he knew about this.

"Later," he said.

We all knelt down. Because the rooms were moving, the downstairs rooms rotated too. There was a room with a piano, the lobby, a dining room, staircases, a luggage closet, and a pool.

"We're on the third floor," I said. "How are we seeing things on the ground floor?"

He took out a small envelope and handed it to me. I took out a purple brass key with a note. It said, *Use 313 escape room at 2200 hours. Destroy upon receipt.*

Clearly, he hadn't destroyed it, but when had he gotten this, and where had it come from? A million questions raced through my head.

"Who gave this to you?" Chloe asked.

"I don't know," he said. "After our meeting, someone left it at my door."

"That's messed up that you kept this from us," Eugene said.

I hissed at Joon, "Did you think you, I don't know, should have told us if some mystery person left you a note? Especially at a hotel where it's supposed to be so private?" I could barely get the words out because I was so angry with him.

Not only was I supposed to be his best friend but we were on a mission.

"Let's get through this alive first," he said, ignoring our questions and pointing to the rooms below us, which were now spinning faster.

"Fine." I was still really mad at him.

Of all the rooms, jumping into the pool seemed like our best option.

I counted in my head as the rooms rotated. "They're switching every nine seconds. I'll time it and start jumping," I instructed. "Chloe, Eugene, Joon, and then I'll go."

Everyone nodded. I started counting aloud. "One, two, three, four, five, six, seven, eight, nine."

"Go!" I shouted.

Chloe jumped in and landed with a splash. Nine seconds later, Eugene jumped in after her.

I put my arm in front of Joon to stop him. "We have to wait for the next rotation."

"Are you okay with jumping into the water?" Joon asked. "I can hold your hand if you want."

I glared at him but counted down in my head. "Stop talking and go!"

He jumped down.

I sat down and after nine seconds pushed off with my arms. The water felt cold. I kicked my legs and swam up to the surface.

Eugene stuck out his hand and helped me out of the pool.

This indoor pool room didn't have any windows, so I couldn't tell what was going on outside. But the columns surrounding the pool began to crumble. And the tiles on the floor heaved up and down.

"Let's get out of here!" Chloe shouted.

We grabbed our backpacks and walked out the door at the far end of the pool.

All the other guests must've left, because there was no one outside. The hotel folded in half and then continued to fold into itself until it was completely gone.

It disappeared right in front of our eyes.

CHAPTER 21

"Where did it go?" I asked. It was dark outside, and there wasn't anything that looked like a hotel as far as I could see.

"The sanctuaries can't be burned down. They're fireproof," Eugene said. "Also, it draws too much unwanted attention if a building blows up."

"There'd be fire trucks and police swarming the place," I said, finally connecting the dots. "But what's the need for the sprinklers if the place was fireproof?"

"That wasn't water," Joon said.

I wiped my face with my hands and studied it. "Looks like water to me."

"It was actually magic holy water, better known as MHW," Joon said. "To ward off evil spirits and monsters."

"But monsters can stay here," I said. "I saw a gumiho by the elevator when we checked in."

"The MHW focuses on evil energy, so the monsters that are allowed to stay here shouldn't be affected," Chloe said.

"If the MHW touched an intruder's bare skin, it would burn them," said Eugene. "Harmless to us."

The textbooks never mentioned anything specific about sanctuary hotels or safe houses, obviously because anyone could read books, and these were secret places for agents in the field. Which was why it was so strange that all three of them knew, even more than I had thought, about them. Umma's warning lingered at the back of my mind and kept me from blurting out everything I was thinking. Joon wasn't sharing about our scary encounter with the man and the billion-won payday. So I kept quiet about that for now. Just until I could figure out who to fully trust.

"I'm going to get out of these wet clothes," I said, and hid behind a tree. "Turn around."

"We're going to change too," said Chloe.

I squatted behind the tree and took clothes and a pair of sneakers out of my backpack, which was completely dry. The IMA-issued ones had a waterproof and a fireproof layer on them. I'd only been out briefly in the rain before, and all the raindrops had just rolled off. I'd worried a little when we'd jumped into the pool with our backpacks, because being submerged underwater was different from some rain, but amazingly the bag had held up well.

After changing into dry clothes and shoes, I wrung out my wet clothes and put them into a wet bag, which automatically dried whatever was put inside. I decided to focus on the new mission. The faster we could get whatever we needed at the other side of the Gureumdari bridge, the faster I could see my parents and share my suspicions with them. Right now, they were the only people I could trust 100 percent.

"All done?" I asked.

"Yeah," everyone shouted back.

I turned around and walked to where we'd been standing before. Everyone looked refreshed. Eugene had a white bandage wrapped around his ankle.

"What happened?" I asked, pointing to his leg.

"Just a little cut from the cords," he said. "They must've rubbed too hard against my ankles."

Joon turned on his phone and dialed the IMA number. He put it on speaker so we could all hear.

"IMA control," said a voice. "State your identities."

Joon cleared his throat and said, "This is Team Air Check."

"Identification number 27401AC9022," I said, reading off the number on our mission document.

"Confirmed," said the voice. "What's the reason for calling?"

"Our sanctuary disappeared," Chloe said. "We are safe."

"Good to hear," said the voice. "Anything else?"

"Yes," Eugene said. "We got cut off earlier and didn't hear the rest of our new mission."

"One moment, please," the voice said, and then Vivaldi's Concerto no. 3 in F Major played in the background.

A few moments later the voice said, "This is highly classified, so it has been sent through a secure message."

"Thank you," Joon said, and hung up.

I turned on my phone, and sure enough, there was a new message alert. When I clicked on the message, laser beams shot out from my phone and scanned my face. The decrypted message said, *Cross the Gureumdari. Retrieve the liquid essences of the four protectors.*

"How straightforward and not cryptic at all," Joon said.

"At least the first part is easy," I said.

We were on a peak of Wolchulsan Mountain. When I opened my map, I saw that the Gureumdari, which literally meant *Cloud Bridge*, was within walking distance from here. The navigation refused to give directions, and only a *Directions Unavailable* message popped up on my screen.

"Navigation isn't working, for some reason," I said.

Eugene took out his compass and asked, "Which direction, Lia?"

"South," I said.

He turned around and said, "This way."

I opened my bag, took out the Ping-Pong balls, and tossed them into the air. They instantly lit up and floated around me.

"Excellent idea," Chloe said.

Chloe, Joon, and Eugene threw their balls up too.

Soon we had little orbs of light surrounding us as we walked.

We trekked along the ridge of the mountain. I could make out something in the distance, but it was too dark to see exactly what it was yet. As we got closer, my jaw dropped open.

It was the longest suspension bridge I had ever

seen, crossing from one mountain peak to another. The reddish-orange bridge had metal mesh sides going all the way across. The bottom of the bridge was supported with evenly spaced horizontal beams.

Now I got why this was called the cloud bridge. It was so high up, I could almost touch the sky.

A strong gust of wind blew, and the bridge creaked and swayed.

"I don't think I can do this," Chloe said as she crossed her arms in front of her.

I put my arm around her shoulder. "It's okay. I'll be right behind you."

She sat down on the grass and began to breathe hard. "I'm deathly afraid of heights," she said, almost in tears.

Joon sat down next to her. "This bridge would make anyone scared."

There was nothing but a bunch of rocks at the bottom of the bridge. It would be an incredibly long fall down and one that no one would survive.

"Maybe you can go without me?" Chloe asked. "Or we could just go back home."

Eugene reached down to pull Chloe up. "Failure is not an option, Chloe. Get up."

I pushed his hand away. What he was saying was true. They wouldn't have sent us on this extra mission if it wasn't important. But forcing Chloe to just get up and go wasn't the way.

"Did you know I used to be really scared of the water?" I said. "Like, I would have a panic attack every time I got into a pool or the ocean."

She wiped the tears from her cheeks. "I never knew that."

Joon nodded and said, "She totally was, a freak-out every single time."

I rolled my eyes. I didn't need him telling her every detail. "But I dug deep and got past it," I continued. "Now I'm okay."

"How did you get over it?" Chloe asked.

"I thought of the people I loved and who depended on me," I said softly. "Maybe you can too?"

She got up slowly. "Okay. I can try."

Eugene was up ahead, checking out the bridge. "It's a little slippery. Just hold on to the railings." He took the first step onto the bridge.

Chloe went next.

"Just keep your eyes focused on Eugene's head," I called after her.

I stood on the bridge and felt it wobble immediately under our weight and from the wind. I reminded myself that this bridge was made of steel, one of the sturdiest materials, and could hold the weight of four kids, no problem.

"Right behind you," Joon said.

We had walked a few more steps when we heard growling.

"Do you hear that?" I stopped and looked around to see where the sound was coming from.

Large wings flapped above me and swooped by.

I ducked. "What was that?"

Chloe froze and clung to the railing. "I can't."

"Weapons out," Eugene yelled. He stood in front of Chloe with his bow drawn.

An owl with large orange wings with black stripes swooshed down. These massive owls were homunjo, a cross between a tiger and an owl—predators.

A homunjo latched on to Joon's shoulder with its talons, and he yelled in pain. I thrust my sword at its wing. The homunjo flapped its wing with such force that I dropped my sword. I dived to the floor to pick it up, but the homunjo shook the bridge with its feet, and my sword slid across. I lunged with outstretched arms and grabbed it right as it was about to fall through a crack in the floor.

"I got you," Eugene shouted to me as he shot an arrow at the homunjo. "Get moving."

"Chloe, you need to move, or we will die," I yelled.

She cried and mumbled, "I can't, I can't, I can't."

"Move," I shouted to Chloe as I held my sword toward the homunjo circling above us.

Eugene grabbed Chloe's arm and pulled her across. When she tried to sit, he picked her up and moved across the bridge.

I made it to the other side of the bridge after them, and Joon followed me. I stood in front of Joon and tried to stop the bleeding by putting pressure on his wound with a towel from my bag.

The homunjo roared and swooshed toward us with its talons out. Chloe and I stood in the front and waved our weapons, while Eugene and Joon stood behind us and fired their arrows into the sky.

They missed.

The owl slashed its claws at Chloe, who stood frozen. I ran in front of her and jabbed the homunjo's chest. It opened its beak and snapped at me. I deflected with my sword. But the homunjo pressed down harder against my sword with its beak.

My legs buckled from the sheer force, and I fell onto my back.

It flew up and then dived down for me with its talons out like daggers. I mustered all my strength and raised my sword.

If I was going to die, I'd never do it without a fight.

CHAPTER 22

Arrows flew through the sky and struck the homunjo on its chest and wings. It stretched and flew away.

We scrambled and hid between some boulders in case it returned. Joon placed his hand on his shoulder and said, "Yakson." His shoulder glowed orange as it healed.

My body shook uncontrollably. I'd really thought I was going to die and that was going to be my ending. If it hadn't been for Eugene and Joon, I'd have been completely slashed to pieces. My chest tightened as I thought about the family and friends I'd have had to leave behind.

Chloe finally spoke up. "I can't believe you all risked your lives for me."

"We have each other's backs," I said.

"Still, you almost died, Lia," Joon said.

"And you and Eugene got the homunjo for me," I said.

I crawled out of our hiding spot and saw only bushes and trees, no clear walking path. "I don't see any liquids here."

Eugene pointed at the trees. "Well, there's only one way to go."

Thank goodness we had each other.

After the dalgyal gwishin yesterday, the last thing I wanted to do was go into another forest.

This time, though, it was a different feeling. Not a feeling of dread but one of peace. As we walked farther into the woods, little sparks of white light twinkled in front of us.

"Should we follow them?" Eugene asked.

Somehow, I knew the answer deep in my soul. "Yes, they're here to help us."

The sparks led the way deeper into the forest. I heard water gushing and felt mist around me. Soon we stood beside a large stream. The lights faded into the water.

A beautiful fairy emerged from the water, wearing a pink robe with a long white sash that floated above her.

"Who are you?" I asked.

Her laugh was musical and soft. "I'm a seonyeo, and you're in my house." She gestured toward the wider area.

"Sorry to bother you," Joon said. "We're here to retrieve the liquid essences of the four protectors."

"And what do you need them for?" she asked.

"To stop the King of Darkness from destroying the world," I said.

She smiled and said, "My, my, that's a big job for such young kids."

"We have to bring the liquids back to IMA," said Eugene.

She nodded and floated down in front of us. "I can help you get started, but the rest is not up to me."

"Then who?" asked Chloe.

"The guardians, of course."

Before any of us could ask what—or who—the guardians were, she raised her hands, and the white sparks appeared again. "Reveal the basins from below."

The white sparks flitted to the stream and dipped inside. Then they flew back and spun four white bowls made out of light.

"Roll your sleeves up and dip your hands inside the bowls," the fairy said.

We pulled up our sleeves and put our hands inside

different bowls. I winced. The scratches on my hand from the homunjo still stung. She raised her hands to the sky and sang, "Guardians, your warriors are here. Grant your essences."

A blue dragon, a red-vermilion bird, a white tiger, and a black turtle appeared in front of each one of us. It was thrilling to finally see the guardian animal representing each of our houses.

The slender blue dragon with long whiskers encircled my arm and then left a blue liquid inside the bowl.

A brilliant red bird fluttered in front of Joon, peered into his face, and dropped a single feather into Joon's bowl and turned it red.

In front of Eugene was the ferocious white tiger with black stripes. It paced around Eugene and then dipped its paw into the water, turning it white.

The black turtle wrapped around Chloe wasn't moving.

"Focus your energy and calm your mind," the fairy said.

Chloe closed her eyes, inhaled, and exhaled. Her knees buckled and her eyes flew open. The black turtle circled her waist and slowly stirred the liquid with its tail, turning it black.

"Warriors, dip your weapons into the essences," said the fairy.

I took my sword out and dipped it inside. The bowl stretched and encased my entire sword. When I took it out, it glowed blue.

Joon's bow and arrows glowed red, Chloe's spear glowed black, and Eugene's bow and arrows glowed white.

Then each bowl of light turned into a glass jar, each with a different liquid inside. I took the one floating in front of me. It looked a bit like a lava lamp, the blue liquid oozing as I turned the jar to the side and upside down.

The seonyeo shot a beam of light out into the woods. "Follow the light, and you'll reach the main road." With that, she disappeared into the water.

"These are so cool!" Eugene said, waving his arrows in the air.

I held my sword in front of me and admired how the blue lit up the dark. "We don't even need to use our Ping-Pong balls," I said.

"Should we rest here for the night?" Joon said.

"It's a long way down." Eugene plopped his bag onto the ground and pulled out a thin mat, which puffed up as soon as he pressed a button.

"That's a cool mat," I said. Wish I had thought to bring an inflatable one too. Instead I had a flat mat and a thin blanket that had a thin layer of heat-trapping material inside to help regulate body temperature.

Chloe lay down on the ground and put her raincoat over herself.

Joon was the best prepared. He took a sack from his bag and stretched it out. It puffed up into a sleeping bag, one of the newest versions.

We placed the four jars in the middle, and they looked like a color campfire, except they didn't give off any heat.

I lay down and clutched my fan on top of me.

"Lia, I never knew your hair was so long," Chloe said.

I touched my head and realized my hair was completely down. Then I remembered I had never tied it back up after dozing off at the sanctuary.

"You should just leave it like that," Eugene said. "The white streak makes you look really cool."

"Much cooler than she actually is," Joon joked.

I grinned. "Thank you." Maybe I'd just leave my hair down a little longer.

They were all the best, and I really didn't want to hide anything from my friends anymore. Sorry, Umma. I needed to tell them what was going on.

I couldn't go to sleep without clearing the air, and my suspicions.

"You know, IMA is really close to finding the eighth identity of the King of Darkness," I said.

"Really?" said Chloe. "I haven't heard anything."

"My mom said it might be someone at our school."

"What?" Eugene said. "How is that even possible?"

"I thought our school was like a fortress," Joon said.

"Well, it's clearly not," I said. "Since even the heirloom got stolen."

"That was strange too," said Chloe. "But you were the last person to hold the paintbrush, Lia."

I couldn't believe she'd gone there. Because we had already established that it wasn't me. So why did she have to bring up the past again?

"Do you think the old woman was right?" Eugene said. "That there's a traitor among us?"

"Me," Joon said jokingly, and raised his hand. "But I apologized, and I haven't done anything since then to make you think that."

"Well, you also got the random note," Eugene said.

"It wasn't his fault that someone anonymously left it at his door," I said in Joon's defense.

"Stop defending him, Lia," Eugene said.

"Don't you think it's strange that someone sent the escape route only to you, Joon?" Chloe asked.

"Maybe someone is looking out for us," I said. "Have you ever thought of that?"

Now was not the time to be blaming and pointing fingers at each other. We had to figure out who the eighth identity at our school was.

"That makes sense too, I guess," Chloe said. "Who do you think it was? "

"No idea," Joon said.

"That wasn't the strange thing about the sanctuary," I said.

"What do you mean?" Eugene asked.

"We were attacked by this man," I explained. "And he kept saying something about a billion-won payout."

They just looked at each other and remained oddly silent.

"What is it?" I demanded.

"You have a bounty on your head," Eugene said slowly.

A what? A bounty? How could I have one? I did absolutely nothing. My power wasn't even working for a while. Why would anyone want to spend that much money on me?

"I don't understand," I said. "How did you all know?"

"There were flyers on the floor of our hallway when the sanctuary went into self-destruct mode," Joon said.

How on earth had I missed that?

"What did they say?" I asked.

"One-billion-won reward, must capture alive," Eugene said.

"That's just so ridiculous," I said in a brave voice. It actually frightened me that someone hated me so much.

"I wonder who put it out?" Chloe said. "You think it was the other team?"

"They were pretty brutal," Joon said.

Eugene shook his head. "You mean your friends? Or are they not your friends anymore?"

Joon grew really quiet.

"Eugene, that's enough," Chloe said.

"I just can't sit back and watch anymore." Eugene turned to me and said, "Lia, you need to wake up and see Joon for what he is."

Now I was getting annoyed, because he was questioning my judgment—or lack of. "See what?"

"You're so blinded by your years of friendship," Eugene said. "You just can't see it, or you're ignoring it."

Chloe pulled at his arm to get him to stop.

"No, it's okay. Let him finish," I said.

"Joon's friends are the ones spreading all those vicious rumors about you," Eugene explained. "And Victor, well, he's the worst."

I couldn't believe what I was hearing. How could Joon

do this to me? I buried my face in my hands and tried to process what Eugene was saying.

Chloe hugged me and pointed at my necklace. "I gave you that because Victor was blocking your magic and making you feel like you were useless."

I couldn't hide my expression anymore. And my face crumpled.

"The necklace I gave you," Chloe continued. "It's a protector against spell blocks."

I hugged Chloe and sobbed. "Thank you." I felt so betrayed by someone who was supposed to be my best friend.

"Lia," Joon said, "I can explain."

I raised my hand and put it in front of his face. "Please just stop talking."

"Fine." He turned his back to me.

"Why don't you get some sleep?" Chloe said. "Eugene and I can take the first watch."

"Thanks," I said, and closed my eyes.

But really, who was I kidding? There were so many thoughts running through my mind that it was impossible to fall asleep. Eugene, Chloe, and I all seemed to agree on one thing.

Joon had been a horrible friend. It was gut-wrenching, but maybe, just maybe, Joon was the one. The traitor.

CHAPTER 23

The sun warmed my body, and I jolted up. What time was it, and how was it not my shift yet? I rubbed my eyes and looked at Joon, fast asleep next to me. I stood up and walked around but saw no sign of Chloe or Eugene.

The jars of liquid that we were supposed to bring back were missing.

This could not be happening.

I shook Joon awake. "Get up!"

He squinted. "Good morning to you, too."

"The jars are missing," I said. "And I can't find Eugene or Chloe anywhere."

"What?" He ran into the woods, yelling for them.

I rolled up my blanket and mat and opened my bag to put them in—and realized that the heirloom was missing. That couldn't be, because I'd made sure to take it out of the safe, and I clearly remembered putting it into my bag along with my sword. I dumped everything out of my bag. There was my badge, pouch, wet clothes, sneakers, toothpaste, toothbrush, Umma's notebook, and phone. But no heirloom.

Joon rushed back from the woods carrying one of Eugene's white arrows. "I pulled this off a tree a little bit down this path."

It was Eugene's, for sure. But what was it doing stuck into a tree? What had he been shooting at?

I stuffed everything back into my bag. "The heirloom is missing."

He turned to stare at me. "Please tell me you're joking, Lia."

"I wish," I said. "I promise I had it in my bag last night before we went to sleep."

This was bad. Not only had we completely failed both missions but we'd also lost two team members, our friends. "We have to call this in," I said.

Joon dialed IMA headquarters on his phone. "It's a busy signal."

That was a very bad sign, because the IMA hotline was never busy or offline.

Maybe normal phone lines were still working. I pressed one to call Umma and breathed a sigh of relief when I heard the line ringing.

She picked up on the second ring. "Lia, is that you?"

"Umma," I said. "We're in trouble. Everything's gone wrong, and I can't get in touch with headquarters."

"Lia, slow down. Headquarters has been taken out," she said. "Where are you?"

What did she mean by that? Like, they'd been physically attacked? Or hacked by a virus so they couldn't operate?

"We're on the other side of the Gureumdari now."

She tapped on her phone and a few seconds later said, "Go down the mountain, and I'll send you an IMA car."

"But, Umma, my friends are missing too. We have to find them first."

"Park Lia," she said. "I need you to listen and get to the car."

"But what about Eugene and Chloe?"

"IMA will send a drone over and we will find them."

"Thank you," I said, and hung up the phone.

I grabbed my bag and said to Joon, "Let's go."

I filled him in on our conversation as we hustled back down. About ten minutes later I saw a black car waiting for us at the foot of the mountain.

"We're almost there," I said.

An ajeossi got out of the driver's side of the car and rushed to help us. "What happened?"

"I don't know," I said. "Our friends are missing."

He opened the rear door and helped us inside.

Once the ajeossi got back into the driver's seat, he said, "Everyone buckled?"

"Before we go," I said, "can you show us identification, please?"

The ajeossi chuckled. "Good for you for asking." He pulled back his ear and rubbed it. The character for *south* appeared. All IMA agents had a secret mark behind their ear.

We both leaned closer and checked. "Thanks," I said.

"It's about a two-hour ride, so just relax," he said.

It was impossible to relax with Chloe and Eugene missing. Were they alive? Who had taken them? Where could they be? And I could potentially have been sitting next to the actual King of Darkness, for all I knew. But then again, it was too obvious a move to take out two of the three people who suspected him. Joon was more strategic than that. If it wasn't Joon, who could it be? Victor was the glaringly obvious choice, but maybe too obvious.

I stared out the window and refused to look at or talk to Joon. Even if he wasn't the traitor, I was still mad at him for everything else. I peeked at him once and grew even madder that he had fallen asleep. I huffed and closed my eyes too.

The two hours crawled by.

When I heard the driver's-side door slam shut, I flung my eyes open. I got out of the car and saw that we had parked right in front of a boating dock facing the ocean.

I couldn't help but admire the stunning view. Along the coastline stood an unending chain of mountains. To the right and inland were small houses and buildings no taller than three stories.

We followed the ajeossi as he walked to the left toward a rocky beach. He continued until we reached a wooded area facing the beach. This was a pretty deserted spot.

"We're almost there," he said as we walked into the forest.

Not even a minute later we came across two large jangseung totem poles.

The one on the right wore a little hat and had

a wide, smiling mouth. On the body was the word *Cheonhadaejanggun*—Great General of All under Heaven. Meanwhile, the jangseung on the left had a long binyeo through her hair, and had the same equally large smile. Inscribed on the body was the word *Jihaeyeojanggun*—Female General of the Underworld. Pairs of these jangseung were always placed in front of villages to ward off evil spirits.

Except there was no village in sight here, it seemed. This was a strange place to build these jangseung, in a forest.

"Welcome to the Village at the End of the World," the ajeossi said. "Or 'Ttangkkeut Maeul' in Korean."

The literal translation of Ttangkkeut Maeul was *Village at the End of the* Land, but I could see how that didn't have the same ring to it. *End of the World* sounded much cooler, though it made me a bit nervous.

I didn't want to be rude because of how eager he sounded to show us this nonexistent village, but I had to ask. "Are you sure we're at the right location?"

Joon rubbed his eyes and blinked a few times. "I don't see a village here either."

"I'd take you in now," he said, "but we're on lockdown, so only people on the inside can let us in."

"I'm not sure about him," I whispered to Joon.

"Me either."

We gave each other a look and inched back slowly so that the ajeossi wouldn't notice. Our other choice was to run, but he had a car and could probably catch up to us pretty quickly. At least if we backed up, we could try to fight him, if it came to that. There were two of us, so I liked our chances.

A bee shot past my face, and I shrieked and batted it away frantically.

The ajeossi yelled and tried to hold my arms. "Stop, stop. Don't touch it!"

Joon pulled me away and stood in front of me with his arms stretched out. "Stay away from us."

The bee flew in between the jangseung, and within seconds a fence appeared. Beyond that I saw white tents, hanok, and people appear out of thin air. It was as if the entire village had been camouflaged.

"Lia?" Umma and Appa raced toward me. Joon's parents rushed to Joon. I hugged Umma and Appa tightly. It felt so good to see them here. "Did you find Chloe and Eugene?" I asked.

"We're using our resources to look for them," Umma said. "I promise you."

Ajumma patted my head and held Joon's hand.

I bowed to greet her. "Annyeonghaseyo."

"I'm so relieved you two made it safely," she said. "See you inside."

Joon and his parents walked past the jangseung.

"How is there an entire village here?" I asked.

"It's cloaked by magic and looks like a giant forest to normal people."

Appa pointed to the fence and whispered, "Only we can see that."

"What happens if people come in here by accident?" I said. It was a pretty remote area, but I could see tourists getting lost and ending up here.

"Sometimes that happens," Umma said. "But once they cross that border, we let loose a flock of crows, who do a wonderful job of scaring them away."

I couldn't stop thinking about Chloe and Eugene. There must have been something we could do to help find them. "Could you tell me what you know so far about where my friends could be?"

Umma sighed. "Let's go inside, and I'll show you what we have."

Right past the white tents near the front of the village was an area with the same kind of platform and low table that we'd seen at the safe house. The kitchen was in a hanok house with a large open front yard. A few people had sat down to eat.

In a fenced outdoor area, about one hundred Hwarang were gathered to train. I recognized a few students from school. It was a big range of ages from adults to kids.

"Are we going to join them?" I asked Umma.

"I probably won't be able to," Umma said. "But you can after we catch you up on some stuff."

I couldn't wait to join later and do what I could to help.

We passed by a sprawling hanok compound. "Ms. Shin, Joon's family, and our family will be staying here." Inside were three separate hanok structures. I followed Umma as she slid open the door to the middle one.

I slipped off my shoes and went inside. There was a living room, kitchen, and one bedroom. It was a traditional-style room so there was no bed. The bedroom was pretty bare except for a giant dresser and a safe. I opened the dresser, and just as I'd thought, there were no mats, blankets, or pillows.

"So I guess we're all sleeping together?" I asked.

"You got it," Appa said. "Family campout."

I loved how he cracked jokes to help take my mind off my missing friends, but it wasn't really working.

"Can we go see if there's an update on Chloe and Eugene?" I asked.

Umma replied, "We were just about to go to a meeting about that."

The meeting was in the compound right next to ours, in a hanok with a silver roof.

Before we even stepped inside, I heard Victor's booming laugh. Sure enough, Victor, Rae, David, and Sena were all there, seated at a long table.

Joon stood by the door with his parents.

Rae ran up to hug me. "I'm so glad you made it out okay."

"You too," I said. "When did you get here?"

"Sometime last night?" she said. "David, what time was it yesterday?"

"Before dinner, so maybe around five p.m.," he said.

Wow. They had us beat, completing their mission early with all four members of their team.

"Heard you lost Chloe and Eugene?" Victor asked.

"We're looking for them," I said.

Victor smirked. "I can't believe they let you go on this mission when you can't even keep each other safe."

"Come on," Joon said. "You know that's not fair. We go on these missions knowing everyone might not make it back."

It was an unspoken understanding that all missions had

this possibility. No matter how careful we were, we could be seriously injured or die. This was exactly why Umma and Appa were considered legendary, because they'd never lost a single person on their group missions, and when it was just the two of them, they always came back.

Victor put his hands up in front of him. "Okay, okay, Joon."

Ms. Shin walked in carrying her laptop and a bag, followed by a couple of other adults I didn't know. "Take your seats, please."

She ran over to Joon and me and hugged us tightly. "Thank goodness you two are okay. By the time I tried to warn you, it was too late."

What was she even talking about? The sanctuary self-destructing or our friends getting kidnapped? Maybe she had sent the note because our phones weren't working. But why wouldn't she have signed the note?

Before I could ask Ms. Shin about it, she hurried to take a seat. I sat down in an empty chair.

Once everyone was seated, Umma pointed to the screen. "Could you run the facial recognition on the main screen?"

"Yes, of course," Ms. Shin said.

She pushed a button on her laptop, and a bunch of photographs of different people flashed in quick succession on the screen. I sat down next to Joon.

"Remember how I told you we tracked down the eighth identity of the nine-headed monster, the King of Darkness, to an individual who was at IMA?" Umma began.

"Did you find the identity?" Joon asked.

"No, not yet," she said. "As you can see, the computer is running different scenarios. But here's the tricky part."

Seven more photographs of people filled the screen. "These are the previous seven identities of the King of Darkness, whom IMA apprehended."

All the photos were of adults, and none looked familiar. I hated the King of Darkness so much in that moment. Why did he have to take innocent people?

"He possesses a human and lives in their subconscious, popping out and controlling the person when necessary. After about twelve weeks of possession, the human is gone, and he has taken full control," Ms. Shin explained.

"And before then?" I asked.

"The human can be saved. Which means we can still save whoever he has possessed," Appa said.

"But how can you be sure that there's still time left?" I mean, no one knew who it was.

"Because there's just no way he could have possessed someone's body while they were at school," Ms. Shin said.

"Because the security is too high," I added.

"Right," Umma said. "So it had to be before."

"But that's still not guaranteed," Joon said. "You're just really hoping it's not too late."

"Yes," Ajumma said. "That is our best-case scenario."

In a span of seconds, this had also turned into a rescue mission. For the first time since I'd gotten here, I had a little hope. "How?"

"We have to kill him," Umma said.

She'd just mentioned the impossible. How were we going to kill a nine-headed monster?

"Thankfully, you have the heirloom and jars of liquid," Ms. Shin said.

"Uh, about that . . . ," Joon said.

I finished the sentence for him. "We lost it all."

Ajeossi put his hands on his head. "That's going to be a problem."

"I'm sorry," I said.

"What were the liquids for?" Joon asked.

"The liquids were essences that only the four guardian animals have," Umma said. "They're made of light, so they can kill the King of Darkness."

"Maybe you can use these." I put my sword on the table, and it still had the blue glow. Joon's bow and arrows still had a red glow.

"Those will work, but they are your weapons and only respond to the owner," Umma said.

"Is there any other way to kill the King of Darkness?" I asked.

"With weapons doused in the four different liquids," she said. "One strike to the heart would kill him."

"I will have to check with the armory here," Ms. Shin said. "But some of our weapons could work in injuring him, even without being doused in liquid."

"Except," Umma said. "We would have to cut off all nine heads." That was very big *except*.

"What about the heavenly heirlooms?" I asked.

"We brought in the dagger," Rae said.

"So we have one," I said. "He has two."

"He will be here to try to steal it," Umma said. "And that will be our opportunity to kill him and recover the heirlooms."

There was just one big problem. "How would the King of Darkness even know the dagger is here?" I asked.

"If he could track it," reasoned David. "We should've run into him during the mission, but we didn't."

The adults all gave one another looks. "We should just tell the kids," Ajeossi said.

"Everyone else in this village already knows," Appa said.

Ms. Shin nodded. "The Pit is located here."

Was she for real? The Pit—as in the dungeon for indestructible monsters? No wonder all the top Hwarang warriors were here. They were preparing for battle.

"Before we come up with a plan," Ms. Shin said, "we're going to have to test everyone here."

"Test us for what?" I asked.

"That the eighth identity of the monster is not among us," Umma said.

This was a brilliant idea and would make it so much easier to work together. At the very least, we would all be able to trust each other.

"How are we going to test?" I asked.

Ms. Shin took a large spray bottle from her bag. "This has magic holy water in it and will burn monsters."

The bottle looked like something that would be used for watering plants around the village. Never would I have guessed that it would be magic holy water.

"Will it hurt?" Rae asked.

"You won't feel a thing," Ms. Shin said. "If you are a regular human being."

"Who wants to go first?" Umma asked.

Nobody raised their hand. I knew I wasn't a monster, but I also didn't want to be the first one sprayed with an unfamiliar substance. What if I had a bad reaction to it? It probably wasn't just water.

Ms. Shin took the bottle and sprayed the water onto her face a couple of times. Then she patted it in. "See, nothing happened. It's actually pretty moisturizing."

Umma volunteered, and Ms. Shin spritzed her face three times. "It's actually a little ticklish and has a refreshing citrus scent," Umma said.

Still no one else volunteered. "I will go around the table, starting with Rae," said Ms. Shin.

Rae pinched her nose with her fingers and squeezed her eyes shut. "I'm ready."

Ms. Shin sprayed her face, and Rae giggled. "It was so much better than I thought it'd be."

David was up next, and he passed successfully as well.

It was finally Victor's turn.

Now was the moment of truth. He seemed a little nervous, and his eyes kept shifting across the room.

Ms. Shin said, "Are you ready?"

"Yes," Victor said.

Just as she was about to spray, a siren went off. Both Ms. Shin and Umma had looks of terror on their faces as they ran outside.

CHAPTER 24

The siren continued to wail, and all the adults grabbed their weapons and rushed to their posts. Umma flew a bee drone into the air. Us kids stood next to her as she piloted it in front of the village.

I picked up the small portable monitor that Umma had left on the ground. I covered my mouth and gasped in horror at the image displayed on the monitor. Two badly bruised bodies were slumped against the jangseung. Just by their clothes, I knew it was Chloe and Eugene. I turned to go to them, but Umma grabbed my arm. "We have to be sure," she said.

Umma flew the drone in to get a better look. The bee

scanned their faces, and their school badges popped up on the monitor.

"They're ours," Ms. Shin shouted. "Unlock the gates."

The gates behind the jangseung completely disappeared.

Joon and I ran outside to find them. Paramedics got there before we did. They must've been stationed near the entrance.

I nodded and picked up Chloe's bag, because there was something sticking out of it. That was impossible. How could she have this? The rattle was stashed inside her bag.

Joon checked Eugene's bag, and within moments he said, "You're not going to believe this," as he pulled out the mirror that had been stolen from our school.

What? Why did Eugene of all people have the mirror? It didn't make any sense, because we were with both of them during the mission. And I'd never once seen that mirror.

Umma had joined us outside and took the mirror and rattle from us. "I'll put the heavenly heirlooms in our safe."

"What's wrong with Chloe and Eugene?" I asked.

"They've been transported to the medical tent," Umma said. "We're going to have to ask them a lot of questions once they wake up. So go wait in your rooms."

She was using her I-mean-business voice, so I walked away. A trilling bell rang, and doctors from one of the tents raced toward the inner part of the village. There must've been an emergency somewhere. It was perfect timing. Joon and I gave each other a look. I surveyed the area to make sure no one was there, and snuck in with Joon, even though I knew it was against the rules.

Chloe and Eugene were lying on beds, and each of them had an IV drip. I hovered over Eugene and placed my ear near his nose to hear if he was breathing.

"Lia," Eugene groaned. "Your face is way too close to mine."

I jumped back and laughed. "So happy you're alive!"

I hugged him, and he winced in pain. "What happened to you two?" I asked.

He rubbed his head and said, "I really don't remember."

Chloe opened her eyes and whispered, "We were on the lookout, remember?"

Eugene nodded. "That's the last thing I remember."

"Can you help me up, Lia?" Chloe stretched out her arms to me.

"You should rest more," I said.

"I just want a little fresh air," she begged.

I helped her up and linked arms with her so that she could lean on me a little as she walked. Once we got outside, she whispered, "I think Eugene did this to me."

Eugene? He was weird sometimes, and he could have a bad temper, but there was no way he would ever hurt or betray us. It sounded silly, but he was a Hwarang who was sworn to protect. I just didn't see him breaking that oath. Plus, he was always the one who was more serious about it than I was.

"I have proof," she added.

"What kind of proof? Where is it?" I asked.

"It's on the heavenly heirlooms," she said. "I planted a recording device on the rattle. You have to be really careful, Lia—I'm pretty sure Eugene is working with a lot of powerful people."

Umma was going to be absolutely livid, but I needed the heirlooms to prove to Chloe that Eugene was not the traitor. Maybe it was Victor or Joon. I mean, how could I trust Victor when he was responsible for spreading all the rumors about me? And Joon had known about it all and had done nothing. Worse than nothing: he'd never even stood up for me. That part hurt the most—that maybe he hadn't because some part of him believed what Victor had been saying.

"I know the code to the safe in my parents' room," I said. "We can just listen to the recording really quickly and put it all back."

"Great plan," Chloe said. "We'll do it so fast that no one will even notice."

I looked at all the people walking around and the cameras literally everywhere in the village. There was no place in this village for us to listen to the recording safely. Because what if by some unlucky chance there was information on there that could hurt Eugene? I wouldn't want it to be permanently on record.

No, we'd have to find a more secure and private location.

"Meet me outside by the water," I whispered to Chloe. "The gates won't be down long."

She looked surprised. "I don't think we should leave this place."

"Well, I can't risk other people hearing this proof that you have."

"Okay," she said. "I'll go out first so that it doesn't look suspicious."

I ran all the way to our compound and quietly opened the door to our hanok. No one was here. Inside our room, I saw the safe. Umma and Appa used the same password for every top secret thing. All our birthdays, in various orders. I punched in 110602250803. It didn't work. I tried 080311060225. The safe unlocked, and I opened it. I took out all three heavenly heirlooms and gently placed them inside my backpack.

I hurried out of there and sprinted past the totem poles. Joon called out my name, but I ignored him and kept going.

Once out of the forest, I headed for the beach with huge black rocks. Chloe was sitting on the sand as the waves lapped near her. I plopped down next to her and handed her my bag.

"It's so peaceful here," she said as she closed her eyes. "Can you hear the waves?"

"Lia!" shouted Joon. I turned around to see both Joon and Eugene running toward us, wildly waving their hands.

Chloe took the heavenly heirlooms out and laid them on the sand.

Joon rushed toward me and whispered into my ear. "It's her."

I stared at him. I couldn't understand what he was telling me.

"She's the baeshinja," Eugene said as he tried to pull me up.

He must've been mistaken. There was no way.

"Chloe?" I asked.

"Look, I won't even touch the heavenly heirlooms." She raised her hands in the air and backed away toward the water.

I picked up the rattle, mirror, and dagger from the ground and handed them to Joon. They floated into the air. The rattle shook, and fireballs shot out from the tips, the mirror twirled and reflected the sun, and the dagger flew straight toward the ocean.

Chloe's eyes turned completely white, and she sneered, "Thanks for activating them."

WHAT?

It *was* Chloe.

She was the eighth identity.

The King of Darkness with all his nine grotesque heads emerged from behind the boulders and caught the dagger in his hand.

A pack of bulgae—fire dogs—appeared next to him.

The King of Darkness pumped the dagger in the air and shouted, "Demolish!"

Some of the bulgae growled and raced into the forest.

"They're headed for the Village at the End of the World," I shouted.

"We have to stop them!" Eugene said.

One of the remaining bulgae pounced into the air, straight at me. I swung my sword and slashed its leg. It yelped and fell to the ground.

Chloe walked into the water and stood frozen in a trance as the waves crashed against her.

Joon and Eugene ran toward her, but the King of Darkness spotted them and used his tail to smack them. They flew through the air and landed a few feet away from me.

I helped them up, and we scrambled as far away as we could.

Joon muttered, "Yakson," and slowly healed a dislocated shoulder.

But Eugene was not in good shape, because he hadn't fully recovered from the earlier attack.

It was up to me to make sure we all got back home safely. I charged with my sword outstretched. *Aim for the heart.*

The King of Darkness laughed and swatted me away with his tail. "Is that all you've got?"

I pressed my sword down in the sand and stood up. Only Joon, Eugene, and I had the weapons doused in the guardian essences, and this was our chance to kill the King of Darkness before he used the dagger to plunge the world into darkness. I was about to draw my sword again to attack when two arrows flew by me, headed for the King of Darkness.

He swatted one away with his arms, and the second hit him in the upper thigh. With a growl, he broke off the part of the arrow that was sticking out and threw it to the ground.

"I totally missed," Eugene said to me, while clutching his leg. There was a large gash there. He must've fallen on something sharp.

We were in the middle of a beach, so there was nothing to bandage his leg with so that it would stop bleeding. As I tended to Eugene, a newly repaired Joon stood up to fight. He shot an arrow at the King of Darkness and started running toward the other end of the beach to lure the nine-headed monster away from us.

I took off my sweater and wrapped it around Eugene's leg.

"No, Lia," he said in a weak voice. "You're going to be so cold."

"I'm going to be running around fighting and winning," I said, patting his chest. "I'll have no time to be cold."

He smiled and fought to keep his eyes open. "I always believed in you. Go get him."

"You need to stop talking," I said, and dragged him a little off the beach to some big rocks. I propped him up against them. "People from IMA are probably already on their way to help. Just hang on, okay?"

"Just go," he said. "I'll be fine."

I clutched my sword and stumbled back onto the beach. It was really hard to run in the sand.

The King of Darkness had arrows stuck in his arm and thigh but had picked Joon up. I sprinted as fast as I could. Speed was key, because there was no hiding from nine heads. I needed to get there before he could react.

I jumped and slashed my sword at him. It sliced through his arm but only on the surface.

But it caused enough pain that he dropped Joon.

I helped him up, and we stood with our backs to each other.

"Bait and switch?" I asked in a low voice.

These were moves we had practiced together back in California, using sticks.

"It's got to be fast," Joon whispered.

I swung my sword at the monster's tail. As the King of Darkness was trying to swing his tail at me, Joon shot an arrow, which hit his shoulder.

The King of Darkness's eyes turned white, and he picked Joon up by the neck.

No way he was going to take my friend. I swung as hard as I could and stabbed his foot.

He howled in pain and angrily threw Joon into the ocean.

I raised my sword in front of me. From the corner of my eye, I couldn't see Joon anywhere in the water.

Then he popped up and stood still, next to Chloe. "What'd you do to them?" I yelled.

"I think I'm going to start a new water statue collection. Don't they look pretty?" the King of Darkness said.

"You're a monster," I yelled.

He knocked me down with his tail and picked me up around the neck. My sword tumbled to the ground and instantly transformed into a fan.

"Wait," I said, trying to buy time. "Before you kill me, at least tell me why you're doing this."

"It was too easy. I slipped into her mind when she was at home," he said. "You have a lot of enemies. I didn't even have to work that hard."

"But why are you trying to kill us all?" I said between breaths.

He loosened his grip ever so slightly, because I think

he wanted me to hear this. Why he hated us all.

"You humans are the worst creations," he said, his voice dripping with disgust. "So much hate, jealousy, and backstabbing that'd you'd make the likes of me blush."

"You're wrong," I said. "Everyone at IMA is a protector to the core."

"Oh really? Did you know that Victor and his group of friends are part of the Magic World Order?"

I paused because I'd actually never heard of such a group before, and I knew all the bureaus and departments within IMA.

As if he'd read my thoughts, he then said, "So naïve. Of course you don't know about them. The Magic World Order believes that IMA and monsters should rule and live side by side."

"Impossible," I said.

That went against everything IMA stood for.

"Why should you have to hide, and sacrifice yourself to protect normal humans?"

Even Victor had standards, I hoped. The King of Darkness was just trying to get me riled up. "No way you could know all that, since you were inside Chloe," I said.

"You think these eight other heads are just spares I like to carry around?" he said. "I can see everything that's going on. And a lot of people have it out for you."

How had this happened? I had totally failed as an agent, because Chloe hadn't even been at the top of my list for being the eighth identity. I'd thought it was Victor, but it turned out he was just mean but not evil. At least I hoped he wasn't evil.

"Enough talk," the King of Darkness said, and threw me onto the ground so hard that I had the wind knocked out of me.

The King of Darkness gripped the dagger and drew a line in the sand until it reached the water. He cackled and said, "Come, my friends. Be free."

Black smoke seeped up from the sand and took shape into different kinds of ghosts and evil spirits. They flew into the sky.

I reached for my fan and yelled, "Idong!" It flew into my hand. I unclasped it and drew my sword, pointing it at the ghosts, but they disappeared with lightninglike speed.

The King of Darkness smashed down with his hands, and I yelled, "Sarajigeora!"

I disappeared for a second and reappeared holding my sword.

That spell had never worked properly before, but

somehow knowing the truth about everything empowered me.

The King of Darkness grabbed me with both hands, and I dropped my sword. I prayed I could finish before passing out, and shouted, "Idong." The sword flew into my hands. I reached down and stabbed straight into his heart.

The King of Darkness fell to the ground with a thud, and I tumbled on top of him. A bluish glow transferred onto his skin. We needed all four of the essences to kill the beast, but it looked like one weapon could temporarily disarm him for a little bit.

Whatever power had been holding Chloe and Joon in place was released, and they waded out from the ocean. I ran to greet them.

She sobbed, "You don't know what it felt like. I fought with myself every day, but I could feel the monster taking over."

"It's okay," I said. "It's over now."

I took Chloe and Joon to where the King of Darkness had been, but he was nowhere to be found.

Just gone.

Ms. Shin, Umma, Appa, Ajumma, and Ajeossi came running toward us.

"Where's the monster?" Umma asked.

"I hit him in the heart with my sword, and then he just disappeared," I explained.

From the rip in the ground, monsters and ghosts continued to seep out.

"No time for talking right now," Umma said. "We need to stop that now."

The adults joined hands. Beams of gold shot out from their hands and sealed the tear in the ground. When it was done, they all collapsed.

I ran to Umma and Appa and helped them sit up. Umma touched my face and said, "Lia, remember how we used to tell you that you were special and you needed to survive?"

I nodded. "I know, because you love me so much."

Umma shook her head. "That, too, of course," she said. "But it's because you are the one spoken of in the prophecy."

Wait a second. That was not what I'd been expecting. What prophecy was she talking about? Surely not the one I knew about the chosen one and all the stars?

"You were born under the Bukduchilseong, and you are destined to be the monster hunter."

I shook my head. "But what if I don't want to be a monster slayer?"

"There's a war coming," she said. "It started years ago, but do you see how things are at a tipping point?"

I guess I did. The King of Darkness was dead set on annihilating the entire human race. If there was more war coming, we'd have to stop it.

"You're the only one who will be able to control monsters," she said.

Actually, that wasn't entirely true. "But, Umma, when the old lady told us about the prophecy, there was an eighth star."

She sighed. "I know, but you are one of the two for this generation."

"Well, who's the other one?"

Umma paused and said softly, "It's Joon."

Joon? My best friend? That couldn't be possible. How could we both be part of the prophecy if he was born more than a thousand years ago?

"When Gaya, his biological mother, placed the mark inside him, it cloaked him from the universe," she said.

As long as he had the mark in him, Joon had grown old like everyone else, except after death, he was always reborn. He had no memories of his past lives. Each cycle of his lives was a clean slate.

Umma continued, "But once Gaya took the mark out

of him, about four months ago, that's when things began to change. The eighth star mysteriously showed up. And the life Joon has now, that's his only one, just like the rest of us."

But there had to be another way. I didn't care what the fortune-teller had said. I wasn't going to fight Joon for this prophecy. "Maybe we could just do it together," I said. "Be monster hunters together."

She looked sad and said, "I wish it were that way, but there's no way of knowing what this kind of knowledge will do to people."

"Well, does Joon know?" I was sure he'd agree with me. That we could now truly be the legendary agent duo.

Umma pointed at Joon, huddled with his parents. "I think they're telling him now."

He looked up at me, and we just stared at each other for a long time.

CHAPTER 25

E ven though there wasn't a single sighting of evil spirits after the epic battle with the King of Darkness, the school pumped up its security measures, created a mandatory buddy system, and informed the students about what to do in case of attacks, and other disasters.

Classes resumed as usual, probably because the school thought routines created a sense of stability. Which fooled no one into believing we were truly safe. The school staff probably felt the same way, because instead of our usual extracurricular activities, all of us were now training harder than ever in either Taekkyeon or Hwarangdo, practicing our magic, and learning about different gadgets and monsters.

The staff must've thought it was safe enough, because today the entire school was at Minsokchon, a Korean folk village attraction nearby, to celebrate the changripginyeomil of our school. Everyone in the magic community knew that it had been a long and hard-fought battle with the Korean government to create a space for our people to practice magic and thrive. In return we protected normal people from monsters.

Lucky for us, International Magic School became that place.

Before we could enjoy our day here, there was one thing we needed to do. We'd made a pact that in our spare time we'd hunt for clues to help Eugene solve the mystery of his missing dad. If it was important to him, it was more than worth it for us.

Because he was our best friend.

But no one seemed to know anything other than that he was dead but the body had never been recovered.

Pretty suspicious.

We huddled around Chloe, who pulled up a black screen on her phone and started coding commands.

Eugene grabbed my hand, and I held Joon's as we waited for Chloe to finish.

Chloe looked up from the screen and smiled nervously. "Ready?"

Eugene gave her a thumbs-up. "Go for it."

Chloe pressed the search button on her phone, and a lot of indecipherable letters and numbers sped up and down the screen.

I clenched my teeth and leaned in to get a better look, though I had no idea what all the random letters meant. Oh, please, please, please let there be a hit this time.

After what felt like an eternity, the screen flashed red, and a notification popped up.

No results found.

Eugene's face was expressionless, but his trembling hands gave away how let down he must've been.

"Are you okay?" I asked.

"If we do more research, I'm sure we could find another clue," Joon said.

"We could try a different keyword next time," Chloe chimed in.

He smiled weakly and spread out his arms to group-hug us. "Thank you."

As if he ever had to ask for my help with anything. "You're my Hwarang brother," I said.

Eugene laughed. "Thanks, sis."

Chloe stretched out her hand, and we piled our hands on top of hers.

"Team Air Check forever," we all shouted.

How much of everything she really remembered, we'll never know. But somehow a part of her recognized us, and we played along. Actually, I desperately wanted to believe that the moments and conversations I'd had with her had been real and it had really been her that I had talked to.

"Something fun now, please," Eugene said.

Joon opened a map and pointed to the red star with a large *You Are Here* sign written in white. "Where to first?"

We were at the entrance to the park and couldn't see any rides. "We should check how long the lines are for the rides we like," I said.

Eugene pointed to a spot on the map. "Let's go here."

"Excellent choice," Joon said.

Before I could ask what ride it was, they bolted.

"Bumper cars," Eugene shouted back.

Ack. How annoying. Did we really have to run during our day off?

Chloe and I jogged behind them.

When we got there, Joon and Eugene were nowhere in sight, but the line circled around the ride three and a half times.

No way we were going to wait that long. I didn't even like the ride that much.

Joon ran up behind us, completely out of breath. "This is the second-shortest line," he panted.

"There's only one ride with a short line," Eugene said.

"The haunted house," said Joon.

Were they serious? After what we'd just gone through? Being around ghosts, even fake ones, was not my idea of fun. It was the last thing I wanted to do right now.

"Let's take a vote," Joon said.

"Raise your hand if you want to go to the haunted house," Chloe said.

I clasped my hands together in front of me.

Joon, Chloe, and Eugene raised their hands.

"Come on, Lia," Eugene said. "We fought the King of Darkness. What is there to be afraid of?"

"I'm not," I replied. "But I don't get why anyone would volunteer to get scared."

Okay, maybe I was also a little frightened. But who

wouldn't be if there was a bounty on your head that went out to the entire monster world?

"Don't worry," Joon said with a wink. "We'll walk in front of you."

Oh my gosh. This wasn't even a ride? We had to actually walk with our own feet through the house? There went my plan for closing my eyes and covering my ears through the whole thing.

Eugene, Chloe, and Joon marched toward a tall traditional Korean gate with blood-red pillars, and passed through it. I groaned and dragged my feet as I trailed behind them.

I stepped into a large courtyard full of barren trees that had skeletons propped up against the trunks. Crows cawed, and a woman's voice shrieked from a hidden speaker somewhere.

It wasn't scary at all. If anything it was a bit cooky and too obvious to be frightening. I mean, the skeletons were obviously fake.

"This isn't so bad," I said, but no one heard me because they had all disappeared into the front entrance of the house.

I couldn't believe they'd gone in without me.

Speed-walk and look straight ahead, I told myself. I'd be out of there in no time.

It was pitch-black inside and eerily quiet.

Once my eyes adjusted, I saw red lights on the ceiling shining down.

Pieces of paper fluttered around me and stayed suspended in the air. I screamed as one landed smack in the middle of my face. I yanked it off and swatted at the ones around me. They dangled in the air.

The unmistakable symbols seen on bujeok glowed red under the light.

All of these pieces of paper were talismans to ward off evil spirits. The haunted house couldn't be that scary if there were bujeok everywhere providing protection.

Just then the bujeok began to burn. Every single one of them.

I ran.

A woman dressed in a white hanbok with long black hair that covered most of her pale white face popped up in front of me. She hissed angrily, "Gajima."

Don't leave.

I screamed and ran even faster.

Something chased me.

Thump, thump, thump.

I refused to turn around and kept running.

The sound grew louder, like someone slowly dribbling a large basketball.

I peeked, and screamed as a headless ghost dressed in a tattered white hanbok yelled, "Nae meori naenoa."

I sped out of there as the ghosts drew nearer. Other ghosts popped up from the sides, but I didn't stop. Not when these ghosts were demanding that I give them their heads.

Suddenly a mass of headless ghosts surrounded me, and something grabbed my arm.

I snatched it away and cringed in pain as something sharp pierced my skin.

I didn't stop running until I burst through the exit into the bright courtyard.

Chloe, Eugene, and Joon were standing nearby waiting for me.

They stared at me with shocked expressions.

"What happened to you?" Joon asked as he rushed over.

"Are you okay?" Chloe asked.

A searing pain shot up my arm, and blood dripped to the ground.

Oh no, no, no.

Everything here was supposed to be fake. How was it

possible that I'd gotten a large gash on my arm?

"Sorry, we should've waited for you," Eugene said.

Yes, they should've, but no one had known that I'd get hurt.

"I'm fine," I said. "My arm must've gotten caught on something while I was running."

Joon reached into his bag and pulled out tissues, a little jar of chopped leaves, and a large gauze, which he handed over to Eugene and Chloe to hold. "Let me see your arm."

I rolled up my sleeve and winced when I saw how deep the gash was.

Joon calmly dabbed the blood with a tissue. "Jar, please," he said.

Eugene unscrewed the cap and handed it to him.

Joon sprinkled the leaves all over my wound.

I cringed because it burned. "What is that?"

"Healing leaves," he said. "I can't heal you myself, but I can get these herbs to do the work for me."

I beamed through the pain. Joon must've been working hard on his craft. This was definitely a level up from the last time I'd talked to him.

"That's so cool!" I said, and tried to pat his arm.

"Thanks," Joon said. "But you need to stay still."

He passed the jar to Eugene, and Chloe handed him the gauze. Then Joon wrapped the white bandage around my arm until it recovered the wound. "Not too tight?"

I wiggled my fingers, which had enough blood circulation so there were no pins and needles. "All good."

"We should tell Ms. Shin about this," Chloe said with a worried look on her face.

If what had scratched me in there was real, then we needed to evacuate this place right away.

Maybe the magic doctors would know what had scratched me by looking at my wound.

"Definitely," I said. "It was probably just a nail or something pointy sticking out, but just in case."

They smiled and pretended to agree with me, but we all knew what it meant when something suspicious happened. Everyone was on high alert these days.

Whatever happened next, even if it was the apocalypse, I was glad I had my friends by my side. Together we'd figure it out and find a way through.

Come what may.

We'd be ready.

Acknowledgments

First, a huge thank-you to all of you for following Lia Park on to her second adventure! I'm delighted and honored to take you into Lia's world of magic and back in time to mystical places in Korea. As Lia discovers more of her power and sense of self, I hope this journey helps you discover the joy of imagination and empowerment.

Penny Moore, my incredible agent, I'm indebted to your unflappable support and enthusiasm for Lia Park, and your brilliance in knowing how to guide authors both practically and emotionally through the art of authoring and publishing. Thank you, thank you, thank you.

Alyson Heller, I don't know how many versions and edits we have gone through, but what I do know with certainty is this: your partnership, your singular talent, and your belief in me and Lia Park were invaluable through my writing journey. Lia and I thank you for every step of the way.

This book wouldn't be possible without the tireless work of so many people. A big thank-you to Valerie Garfield, Kristin Gilson, Anna Jarzab, Ginny Kemmerer, Michelle Leo, Amy Beaudoin, Lindsey Ferris, Lisa Quach,

ACKNOWLEDGMENTS

Sara Berko, and the entire team at Aladdin and Simon & Schuster.

Hyuna Lee, I often wondered how the essence of Lia, her heritage, and her adventures could possibly be captured in one image. Yet again, your stunning cover somehow brought the book to life in ways I had always hoped but could never imagine. Heather Palisi, thank you for designing another gorgeous jacket and bringing the words and images to life. Thank you so much.

I will always have the deepest gratitude and respect for educators, librarians, and booksellers, who are integral in enabling children to read and learn. Thank you for your love for Lia Park and for all that you do.

Life and this journey would be altogether different and lacking without family and friends who have generously shown me love, support, and encouragement. I am so grateful for your friendship, and of course, for all the times you've recommended and gifted the Lia Park books to others.

Momma friends have a special place in my heart. My Texas crew, Angela and Yijing, your friendship and welcoming arms when our family first moved to Texas will always stay with me. And I know if you were not around to take care of my children when we all got sick (these

ACKNOWLEDGMENTS

are the times!) while I had to write, this book would have had a different outcome. Thank you so much.

My Zoomies, Miri and Sanli, thank you for another year of uplifting conversations and continued prayers and support. The kind of friendship we have is rare, and I am grateful for you every day. Thank you for years of friendship across time zone changes and state lines.

To my mother- and father-in-law, I am strengthened and buoyed up by your love and support throughout the years. Thank you for treating me like your own daughter, and for being my second set of parents. To have this sort of love is a blessing I cherish.

To Jee Hae and Eddie, your constant encouragement and support made this journey that much easier. Thank you, Eddie, my coffee buddy, for driving me around NYC to all the independent bookstores. Thank you, Jee Hae, for being my best friend since day one, for always being there for the big and small conversations, and for being my biggest cheerleader. The best sister one could ever have.

To my Umma and Appa, I will always remember our epic road trip through Korea with the girls. Thank you for traveling with me to all the locations in this book and for building beautiful core memories for the girls in their mother's motherland. Umma, thank you for being my

ACKNOWLEDGMENTS

enthusiastic mountain-climbing partner—I'm so proud
that we made it to the top. Appa, thank you for encour-
aging me even before I could write, and telling me that I
could pursue all my dreams. Umma and Appa, Lia Park
would not exist without your endless love, support, and
belief in me. Thank you.

My darling Mihee and Taehee, you two are my inspira-
tion, my greatest joy, and the reason I write. Reach for the
stars, my loves. Always dream big, never stop being you,
and remember magic lives within you. I love you to the
galaxies and beyond.

My dear Bud, to do life with you is a wonderful adventure and my best decision. Thank you for being my sup-
portive rock and my greatest thought partner, and for
making me laugh every single day, no matter what the
circumstance. To have not just the best husband but to
see you also be the best father will always move my heart.
Thank you, my love.

Thank you, God, for your grace, blessings, and for
being my strength and hope through it all. I am who I am
because of you.

About the Author

Jenna Yoon studied art history at Wellesley College and received her master's degree in Korean art history from Ewha Womans University. She's lived about half her life in Korea and half in the United States. When she's not writing, Jenna loves to travel, find yummy eats, and play board games, and she takes skin care very seriously. She lives in Austin, Texas, with her husband and two kids. For more information, visit her website at AuthorJennaYoon.com, or follow her on Instagram and Twitter @AuthorJennaYoon.